"How are you doing, Abby?"

Nick was watching her over the gate. Without being invited, he vaulted over it into the garden.

Abby was mad that she'd remembered his features in detail, but she'd forgotten his subtle way of dominating his surroundings. She said the first thing that came into her head.

"So you decided to come after all."

Nick grinned. "Sure. Were you hoping I'd changed my mind?"

"It had occurred to me." Abby took refuge in her haughty air.

"Tough luck, Abigail. I'm here for the duration." She took a step backward, losing her footing on the edge of the border. His strong hand shot out to catch her.

"Falling over herself to greet me," he murmured, laughter in his eyes.

Jessica Hart was born in Ghana, but grew up in an Oxfordshire village. Her father was a civil engineer working overseas, so by the time she left school, she'd been to East Africa, South Africa, Papua New Guinea and Oman—and had acquired incurably itchy feet. After spending a year in New Zealand with a cousin, where she says she learned a thousand things to do with mutton, she studied French Literature at Edinburgh University, graduating in 1981. Since then, she's had a haphazard series of jobs—production assistant at a theater, research assistant, waitress, teaching English, cook on an outback property—in England, Egypt, Kenya, Jakarta and Australia, respectively. She's also worked with Operation Raleigh, selecting Venturers for expeditions, which took her to Cameroon and Algeria. At present, she works as foreign newsdesk secretary at the *Observer,* but eventually, she wants to leave London and take a further degree in Medieval history. This is her first Harlequin Romance novel.

A SWEETER PREJUDICE
Jessica Hart

Harlequin Books

TORONTO • NEW YORK • LONDON
AMSTERDAM • PARIS • SYDNEY • HAMBURG
STOCKHOLM • ATHENS • TOKYO • MILAN

Original hardcover edition published in 1991
by Mills & Boon Limited

ISBN 0-373-17099-8

Harlequin Romance first edition December 1991

For Diana and Miles

CHAPTER ONE

ABBY leant on the handlebars and squinted downhill to where the village of Stynch Magna drowsed in the distant summer haze. It looked like being a long walk home.

Still, she shrugged philosophically, there were worse places to have a puncture. Her grey eyes lingered on the rolling patchwork of the Oxfordshire countryside spread out below her and she breathed in appreciatively, savouring the peculiar stillness of a hot summer afternoon. Putting the walk ahead out of her mind, Abby turned her face up to the sun with a contented sigh and let her thoughts drift.

The roar of an approaching car shattered the tranquillity of the afternoon, and Abby opened her eyes with a frown at the intrusion. Why was it that whenever you found a peaceful spot, some idiot in a car had to come along trailing noise and fumes to spoil things? Whoever it was was coming far too fast by the sound of it, too, she thought, and she pulled the bike further on to the grassy verge, careful to avoid the poppies whose scarlet heads dipped and swayed in the light breeze.

She prepared to glare as a huge open-topped Rolls-Royce loomed over the crest of the hill. Somebody else who thought they owned the road just because they had an expensive car! The car started to accelerate down the hill, but at the sight of Abby standing knee-deep in poppies the driver obviously changed his mind and brought the car to a skidding halt in front of her.

'Hi, there!' With his striking dark good looks, designer sunglasses and matching tan, the driver looked as if he had stepped out of the pages of a glossy magazine. One hand rested lightly on the steering-wheel as he leant over the door and smiled at Abby in a way that would have had most female hearts turning somersaults.

Not Abigail Smith's, though. She had stiffened at the unmistakable American accent and looked back at him frostily.

'This is a bit of luck.' He took off his sunglasses and Abby found herself staring into a pair of wickedly green eyes. Her heart, which had remained so admirably still before, reacted now with an alarming handspring, hurriedly suppressed. This was just another tourist, after all. But his eyes danced with an intelligence and humour that somehow brought the hard, exciting lines of his face into sharper focus and left Abby feeling oddly winded, as if by an unexpected blow. She took a steadying breath. *Just another tourist.*

'I wasn't expecting to meet anyone on this road,' he was saying.

'No doubt that's why you were driving so dangerously,' Abby said pointedly, trying to will her pulse-rate into submission.

The latent laughter sprang readily to his eyes. '*Was* I driving dangerously?'

'Yes, you were. You were driving much too fast, anyway.' Abby was unsettled by the sheer force of personality of the man, and dragged her eyes away from his in an effort to stay cool and collected. She was not the kind of girl to be bowled over by a handsome face, and annoyance at her unexpectedly physical response—and to someone who already seemed to represent everything she disliked and distrusted most!—sharpened her voice. 'If there'd been a rabbit or something sitting in the middle of the road, you'd have killed it as you came over that hill. Come to that, I could have been sitting in the middle of the road.'

The American pretended to consider her point, but she knew he was laughing at her. 'Why would you be sitting in the middle of the road?'

'*I* wouldn't, but a rabbit might be.'

He scratched his chin. 'I'm sorry, you've lost me. . .'

'The point I'm trying to make,' Abby said, steeling herself against his almost tangible charm, 'is that a rabbit has just as much right to be in the road as you do, and it doesn't deserve to be killed just because you feel like putting your foot on the accelerator.' She flushed slightly, realising that she must sound ridiculous.

'I hadn't thought about rabbits' rights before, but I can see you're right,' he said, deadpan, and Abby bit her lip. Why had she started going on about rabbits? He probably already had her written down as an English eccentric.

As if taking pity on her, he went on, 'I guess I was going a bit fast, but I'm late, I'm lost. . .and this old girl has brakes like you wouldn't believe!' He patted the steering-wheel affectionately and added in a confidentially chatty voice, 'I always wanted to drive one of these round England. Isn't she beautiful?'

The blithe charm and instant friendliness brought back bitter memories. The American radiated such energy and exuberant enjoyment of life that the gentle softness of the surrounding countryside seemed dimmer by comparison.

'If you like that sort of thing,' said Abby, who had secretly always dreamt of owning just such a timelessly elegant car. Its dark racing green bodywork appealed to her too, but something about the American had set her on the defensive, and she went on in a deliberately cold voice, 'Personally I find them vulgar, and quite unsuitable for these country roads.'

'Hey, that's *me* put in my place!' Unabashed, he grinned, his teeth very white against his tan, and looked at Abby with renewed interest. She was a tall, willowy girl, with a pair of unnervingly direct grey eyes and a deceptively aloof expression which sometimes gave her an old-fashioned air. She had piled the mass of glossy chestnut hair on top of her head for coolness, but, as the amusement in his green eyes deepened, Abby became uncomfortably aware of it escaping in the heat. It had been a long, hard ride to the top of the hill, and her face was still flushed with effort.

Annoyed by his scrutiny, Abby pushed the wayward strands behind her ears and glared back at him.

'Sorry, was I staring? You just looked so English standing there with your nose in the air!' He didn't sound at all apologetic, Abby thought angrily, as he breezed on, 'I'm real glad to see you, anyway. I feel as if I've been driving round in circles on these roads— oh, for a straight American highway!' He picked up a map from the seat beside him. 'The truth is, I'm lost. Could you show me exactly where I am now?'

She could hardly refuse, she supposed. Rather reluctantly, Abby lifted the bike back on to the road and pushed it over to where the American was spreading the map open over the vast bonnet. He was taller than she'd imagined, and his powerful build was thinly disguised by the vividly patterned shirt he wore tucked casually into his jeans. He obviously liked his clothes as loud as his personality, Abby thought unfairly, ignoring the fact that everyone was wearing bright clothes that summer.

She was very aware of him as she bent her head over the map and tried hard to concentrate on the maze of yellow and white lines. 'You're here.' Grudgingly, she pointed the place out with her finger.

He peered over her shoulder. 'No kidding? How did I end up there? I was trying to get to a place called. . .' He consulted a scrap of paper. 'Stynch Magna. Some name, huh? Is that far from here?'

Abby hoped her surprise didn't show in her face. What on earth would a man like this want in Stynch Magna? 'About five or six miles,' she said in a cool voice and gestured down the hill. 'You just go straight down this road, right at the first crossroads and then left when you get to the T-junction.'

'Great.' He glanced at his watch. Abby noted with surprise that it had an old leather strap. She would have thought an ostentatious gold one would be more his style. The watch, like the beautiful car, seemed out of keeping with the man. 'I shouldn't be too late, then.'

She longed to ask who this American was going to see, but would have died rather than show any interest. In any case, she reflected, she would hear about it soon enough. Nothing remained secret for long in such a small village.

'Where are you on your way to?' he asked as he folded up the map.

'Home,' said Abby uninformatively.

'Can I give you a ride?'

'No, thank you. I have my bike.' Abby was coldly polite.

'Are you sure? That back wheel doesn't look too hot.' Before she could stop him, he had bent to examine the tyre. 'Yep, you've got a flat there.'

She gritted her teeth. Why didn't he stop interfering and go on his way? 'I'm aware of that.'

'It'd be no trouble to throw the bike in the trunk.'

'I'd rather walk.'

He straightened to look down at her, evidently puzzled by her unfriendly attitude, but there was a dangerous twinkle in his green eyes that set Abby's treacherous pulse strumming once more. Fiercely she suppressed the warmth that seemed to uncoil deep inside her in response, and was glad to hide behind her mask of chilly hauteur. 'I could drop you off before anyone saw you in such a vulgar car!' he persevered.

Abby favoured him with a look and the twinkle deepened. 'No? I guess it must be me after all.' He tossed the map into the car and then swung himself lightly over the door. 'Thanks for your help, anyway.'

Why couldn't he open the door like any normal person? Abby wondered crossly. She inclined her head in stiff acknowledgement.

'I'll watch out for the rabbits this time,' he called as the engine purred into life.

'Please do,' Abby retorted in what she hoped was a quelling manner.

To her chagrin, the American merely burst out laughing. 'Quite a little duchess, aren't we?' He shook his head and settled his sunglasses on his nose. 'You Brits!' Letting out the clutch, he gave her a cheery wave—'Bye, duchess!'—and shot off with a deliberate squeal of tyres, still laughing.

Abby stared after him resentfully. How she loathed that particular brand of superficial charm! Suddenly overwhelmed by memories of Stephen, she sat down on the grass verge and stared blankly at the road where the Rolls had stood in all its gleaming magnificence. The road seemed very quiet and oddly empty without it, or its obnoxious driver.

The American's face, with its infuriating expression of complacent amusement, rose before her. At least he wouldn't be staying in Stynch Magna, she comforted herself. There was nothing there to interest an American for more than the time it took to take a photograph. After all, that was one of the reasons she had chosen it.

By the time she reached the village, Abby was hot, thirsty and irritable. It had been a longer walk than she had thought and her sandals, perfectly adequate for cycling, had left her feet blistered and aching. The thought that she could have saved herself the trouble by accepting a lift from the American did not improve her temper.

The sight that met her eyes as she turned wearily at last into the lane stopped her dead in her tracks with an odd leap of the heart. Not only was the Rolls-Royce

here, of all places, but it was parked right opposite
Meadow Cottage!

Normally the sight of her cottage gave Abby a warm
thrill of possession. It was, she was the first to admit,
a very modest abode. One of a pair of cottages under
one roof, it was half the size of its neighbour, with
only two tiny rooms upstairs and two more below, but
to Abby it represented all she had ever dreamed of.
An old-fashioned girl in an old-fashioned house,
friends teased, but Abby didn't care. The old stone
walls seemed to grow out of the ground, lumpy and
leaning with age, and in the late afternoon sunshine
they gave off a mellow golden glow. The original
thatched roof had burnt down many years before, and
now tiles united the two cottages, but that was the only
concession to symmetry. All the windows were of
different sizes, and while Mrs Walker's front door was
shaded by a porch over which scrambled a luxuriant
blue wisteria, Abby was content with a plain wooden
door opening on to the path, giving the cottages a
decidedly lop-sided effect.

But now, as she pushed her bike slowly forward, the
big car with its distinctive racing green seemed to
throw everything out of proportion. It looked ridiculously out of place parked on the verge, and brought
back a vivid memory of laughing eyes and an unsettling
warmth. Abby glanced up and down the lane, unable
to imagine anyone who might have been expecting
such an incongruous visitor, but, apart from the distant
clatter of a lawnmower, all was quiet and the serene
faces of the cottages gave nothing away.

Still, it was nothing to her *who* the American chose
to visit, Abby convinced herself. With a shrug, she

propped her bike against the wall and stepped into the quiet cool of the stone-flagged hallway. Pouring herself a cold drink from the fridge, she went to sit in her favourite position on the kitchen doorstep, and smiled as a big tabby emerged yawning from beneath the rose bushes to greet her. Elijah never failed to welcome her home. Even though she lived alone, Abby never felt lonely with his undemanding company. She scratched him behind his ear, and he rolled his shoulders in appreciation.

'There you are!' Abby looked up to see Letty Walker beaming at her over the wall that divided the two gardens. 'Do come and have a cup of tea, dear. There's someone I want you to meet.' She unlatched the wooden gate invitingly. 'I've been looking for you all afternoon. Where have you been?'

'Delivering a painting to Mannerton.' Abby smiled wearily at her elderly neighbour as she limped over to join her. 'Only I got a puncture and had to push the bike all the way back from Cobb Hill.'

'Dear me, you must be exhausted.' Mrs Walker clicked her tongue with sympathy. 'Never mind, a nice cup of tea will do you the world of good.'

A nice cup of tea was Letty Walker's panacea for all ills, and Abby couldn't help smiling as she allowed herself to be ushered into her neighbour's immaculate cottage garden, only to feel the smile freezing on her face as she saw who had risen to his feet to meet her.

Abby was totally unprepared for the way the breath caught in her throat at the sight of the American again. Her heart seemed to have jolted into a life of its own, and for a moment she could only stare at him while it battered against her ribs like a trapped bird. He looked almost aggressively masculine, lean and dark against the softly pretty background of Mrs Walker's prized herbaceous border. The car outside should have been warning enough, but she had somehow never expected to find him here, with Letty Walker of all people!

His eyebrows had lifted in surprised recognition, but now he smiled down at her as he came towards her, his eyes alight with laughter. 'Well, well, if it isn't the duchess!' he said softly.

Letty Walker bustled past Abby to set out another garden chair. 'Here's Abby at last! Abby, this is Nick Carleton.' She beamed at them both, and Abby had no choice but to shake his outstretched hand.

'How do you do?' she said stiffly, withdrawing her fingers from his cool, strong clasp as if they'd been burnt. It was just surprise, of course, but she wished her heart would stop jumping around like that, and she took a deep, steadying breath.

'How do *you* do, Abigail?' he mimicked her gravely. 'Guess I'd better learn to talk British if I'm going to spend a summer over here!'

Talk British! Abby winced involuntarily as she took a seat at the wooden table set in the shade of an apple tree.

'Poor Abby's had problems with her bicycle and has had to walk miles,' Letty said to Nick, adding to Abby, 'You'd think someone would have given you a lift.'

'People can be so unfriendly, can't they?' said Nick. Abby looked up quickly and for a second grey eyes clashed with green. He must have noticed the way she was limping on her blistered feet.

'Anyway, you made it back in time to meet Nick,'

Letty carried on happily as she poured a cup of tea for Abby. 'It would have been such a pity if you'd missed him.'

'Awful,' Abby murmured, wishing she'd had to walk another five miles, anything to avoid seeing this smug American again. Opposite her, Nick lounged in his chair and watched her with amusement. She had the uncomfortable feeling that he knew exactly what she was thinking and she wondered why he hadn't mentioned that they had already met. Sipping her tea, she glared back over the rim of the fine china cup. What was he doing here, anyway?

'You and Nick are going to be neighbours for the summer, Abby.' Letty Walker answered her unspoken question, and serenely handed Nick a plate of scones.

'*What*?' Abby choked on her tea and put her cup down with a clatter, staring at Letty with undisguised horror. On the other side of the table, Nick applied himself to buttering his scone and suppressing his grin.

'I don't know what you're so surprised about, dear,' Letty said, faintly reproving. 'It was your idea, after all.'

'What?' Abby said again in a strangled voice.

'Well, dear, it was you who suggested that I try to rent out the cottage while I'm in Australia with Margot.'

'Yes, but. . .' Abby trailed off. She had envisaged some little old lady, not an American, and certainly not an American like Nick Carleton.

'It's all worked out wonderfully. Nick is going to move in as soon as I fly out, and look after the cottage for me.'

He didn't look much like a man who knew much

about housekeeping, Abby reflected. Fast cars, fast women and nightclubs, maybe, but country cottages—no!

'I'll certainly do my best,' he was saying modestly. 'Delicious scones, Letty.'

Creep, thought Abby. What on earth had possessed her to suggest that Letty rent out the cottage while she visited her daughter? She could have had a nice quiet summer. It wouldn't have been any trouble to look after Letty's cottage, and, although her neighbour would undoubtedly appreciate a little extra income, would it be worth having a complete stranger in her home? Abby glanced at Nick under her lashes again. He looked dangerously out of context in this timeless garden. Attractive, yes—she was uncomfortably aware of that—but who was he, after all?

'When did you decide all this, Letty?' she asked carefully. What if the old lady had got herself in the hands of some confidence trickster? It wouldn't be the first time, and few people would be proof against the vibrant charm of a man like this.

'Yesterday, at the Simpsons'. You remember them, don't you, dear? They came to lunch here in January—or was it February? Their son's always been such a clever boy, and now he's working in Hollywood of all places! He's a. . .what is he, Nicholas?'

'A screenwriter,' Nick supplied gravely. 'Alan's a good friend of mine, and, when he knew I was coming to England, he asked me to look up his parents. I'm real glad I did. I'd been thinking about spending the summer over here, and when Letty here came over and told me about her cottage standing empty all summer. . .well, it seemed like the perfect opportunity to get away from it all.'

'Get away from all *what*?' Abby asked nastily before she could stop herself.

Nick shot her a disconcerting green glance before accepting another scone from Letty with a self-deprecating shrug. 'The last two or three years have been rather busy,' he said mildly.

Abby had the impression he was about to say more, but at that moment the shrill call of the telephone echoed from inside the cottage and Letty fluttered off to answer it. Abby and Nick were left staring at each other in unspoken challenge.

'You don't like me, do you, Abigail Smith?' he said eventually.

'I don't know anything about you.' Abby brushed the crumbs off her skirt, glad of the excuse to look away from those unsettling eyes. 'I just don't want anyone to take advantage of Letty. She doesn't really know you—nor do the Simpsons, come to that. You might be a con man or an escaped lunatic for all we know. I mean, who *are* you?'

Was it her imagination, or did he hesitate slightly? 'I'm an actor.'

Of course, they all said they were actors! Abby raised her eyebrows in polite disbelief. 'Oh, really?'

'Yes, *really*!' He had beautiful teeth, strong and white. His smile, slow and warm, seemed to start in his eyes and was very slightly crooked. Abby found herself noticing how it deepened the crease in his left cheek and looked hastily away.

'Well, I'm going to try to find out more about you

before Letty hands you the keys to her cottage,' she said, recollecting herself.

'Sure,' he said equably. 'I'm delighted you're so interested in me.'

'I'm *not* interested in you,' Abby replied in an icy voice. She had herself well under control now. 'I'm interested in seeing that Letty doesn't get hurt, that's all.'

'You know, you're not at all the way I imagined you,' Nick said abruptly.

'Oh?' Abby lifted her chin. 'And how was that?'

He looked her over consideringly, taking in the wary grey eyes, the proud tilt of her head and the skin warm as amber in the early evening light. 'Letty told me there was a very nice, sensible girl next door who'd look after the garden. I thought you'd be all brisk and bossy and hearty laughter.' There was that smile again. It was definitely crooked. 'Yeah, I figured you'd be one of those girls with too many teeth and terrible legs. You're a nice surprise, Abigail Smith—even if you are snooty!'

Abby flushed and set her teeth. 'Your line is obviously more effective with old ladies than it is with young ones, Mr Carleton!' She tried to sound cutting but Nick merely laughed with such obvious amusement that Letty, hurrying back to her guests, settled back into her chair with a satisfied smile.

'I'm so pleased you two are getting on together!'

It was so inappropriate that Abby, much to her own dismay, was unable to resist an answering smile to the gleam in Nick's green eyes. For a moment her face lit up with amusement, allowing him a glimpse of sparkling warmth before the chilly mask of hostility dropped back into place. Unaware of Nick's suddenly arrested expression, Abby picked up her cup of tea and concentrated on it fiercely, confused by that unexpectedly shared flash of humour. It was as if he had reached out and touched her, an almost tangible recognition between them that was almost more disturbing than her dislike.

'I'm sure you'll have lots in common,' Letty chattered on comfortably. 'You spent quite a long time in America, didn't you, dear?'

Abby's lingering half-smile vanished. She didn't want to talk to anyone about her time in the States, least of all Nick Carleton.

'Yeah?' He leant forward with interest. 'Whereabouts?'

'Washington,' she said shortly.

'Really? On holiday?'

'No.' Abby stared unseeingly at a bee hovering industriously among the delphiniums, and her grey eyes darkened at some memory. 'No, not exactly. My mother remarried, to an American, and I was staying with them.'

As if sensing that she did not want to pursue the subject, Nick asked no more questions, and to her relief Letty changed the subject.

'By the way, that was Peter on the phone just now, Abby.'

'Oh?' Abby looked wary. Peter Middleton was the local estate agent, whose determined wooing had become something of a village joke. 'What did he want?'

'Funnily enough, I'd mentioned to him about letting the cottage, and he'd just had a phone call from someone interested in renting, but of course, I was able to tell him I already had a tenant.' She smiled at Nick fondly, adding, as an afterthought, 'He said he'd drop round to see you this evening. I told him you were here. Such a *suitable* young man!' She looked at Abby hopefully.

Abby suppressed a sigh. Mrs Walker was determined to see her married off as soon as possible.

'Who's Peter?' Nick asked; not showing the slightest embarrassment at asking personal questions, Abby thought indignantly.

Sensing an ally, Letty Walker ignored Abby's warning frown. 'Peter Middleton is Abby's young man, and it's high time she paid him more attention. Husbands don't grow on trees, dear!'

'Peter is *not* my young man,' Abby protested in anguished embarrassment, acutely aware of Nick's interested gaze.

'Nonsense, dear, the boy's head over heels in love with you, and you ought to spend more time with him instead of looking after troublesome old neighbours.'

In spite of her vexation, Abby's face relaxed into a fond smile. 'You're not troublesome, Letty.'

'I'm sure I am.' She turned to Nick. 'You've no idea what a help Abby's been to me since Gerald died. She practically bullied me into this trip to Australia and made all the arrangements for me. I don't know what I'd have done without her.'

Abby flushed uncomfortably. 'I hardly did anything, Letty.' Pushing back her chair, she got to her feet. 'I must go. Thank you for the tea.'

Nick stood up too. 'It's been a pleasure meeting you, Abigail.' His green eyes danced. Even when his expression was quite serious, as now, Abby had the disconcerting feeling that he was laughing at her. 'I'll see you in a couple of weeks, I hope.'

So soon! Abby wondered if her dismay showed in her face. She merely gave him a distant nod—no doubt *he* would call it a snooty nod—and turned away, and the American had the last word.

'By the way, good luck with your enquiries!'

Abby had thought she would ring the Simpsons to find out how much they knew about Letty's new tenant, but she was still trying to think of a way to get their phone number from Letty without confessing her misgivings when she learnt all she needed much closer to home in the village shop. She was half-heartedly searching the lower shelves for Elijah's favourite brand of catfood when she heard a name that made her straighten and stare over to where her friend Liz was gossiping with the shop assistant.

'*Who* did you say?'

'Nick Carleton.' Liz looked puzzled at her tone.

'How do you know about him?'

'Really, Abby, everybody knows about Nick Carleton!' From behind the counter, Sarah flicked a swathe of blonde hair over her shoulder. 'Isn't it exciting?'

Abby put her basket down carefully. 'What do you mean, everybody knows about him? Who is he?'

Liz and Sarah looked at her in astonishment. 'Even you must have heard of Nick Carleton!'

Abby began to have an odd feeling in the pit of her stomach. 'Tell me.'

'Honestly, Abby, sometimes I think you must live in a time warp!' Liz turned to Sarah in exasperation. 'She doesn't watch television, she doesn't go to the cinema, she doesn't listen to pop music. . .I keep telling her life's too short for good taste the whole time, but she doesn't take any notice.'

'What about Nick Carleton, though?' Abby ignored Liz's familiar lament.

'He's *the* big name in Hollywood at the moment,' Sarah explained importantly. 'He was in *The Summer House* last year—that was a brilliant film—and he's on telly. He's Carver in that thriller series on Wednesday nights. You *must* have seen it, Abby!'

'And he's in that new film everyone's talking about, *Tomorrow You Die*. It should be coming to Turlbury soon. I can't wait to see it.' Liz paused and looked closer at her friend. 'Is something the matter?'

Abby shook her head absently. It couldn't be. . .could it? 'What does he look like?'

'Gorgeous! Here, I'll show you.' Sarah rummaged beneath the counter, re-emerging triumphantly with a much-handled cutting from a magazine, which she handed to Abby. 'NICK CARLETON—MAN OF THE MOMENT' ran the heading.

There was no mistaking him. No mistaking the darkly handsome features, the mobile mouth or the devastating smile. No mistaking her jolting response, either. Making a great effort to breathe normally, Abby stared down at the photograph, which showed Nick leaning casually against a wall, arms folded across his broad chest. There was an aggressive vitality about him that somehow transcended the cheap, shiny paper of the magazine and recalled all too vividly the way those green eyes had laughed into hers.

The same smug expression too, Abby decided. No

wonder he had been so amused! She remembered how she had been so obviously disbelieving when he'd told her that he was an actor, and cringed inwardly. He must have known that she would soon find out how famous he was.

'Isn't he gorgeous?' Sarah sighed again, craning her neck to gaze wistfully at the picture. 'Gosh, I hope this rumour that he's coming here is true.'

'It is,' Abby said in a hollow voice.

The two girls stared. 'How do you know?' they asked in unison.

'I met him,' she explained as nonchalantly as she could manage, handing the cutting back to Sarah. 'He's moving into Letty Walker's cottage while she's in Australia.'

'You're kidding!' Sarah stood open-mouthed, the cutting forgotten in her hand.

Abby began to stack her shopping on the counter. 'I only wish I were!'

'But. . .but. . .Abby, you lucky thing!' Liz was obviously having trouble taking in the news. 'Why didn't you tell me you'd met him?'

'I didn't know who he was,' Abby said defensively. 'I'd never heard of him, and I'm sure Letty hasn't either. If he'd been a famous gardener, it might have been a different story.'

'Well, go on.' Sarah began writing Abby's purchases in the account book, but her mind was on other things. 'What's he like? Is he as good-looking in real life?'

'Oh, yes, and doesn't he know it!' Abby said sourly. 'He's certainly not my type. I prefer intelligent, articulate men.' As if aware that she sounded unconvincing, she added, in a carefully dismissive voice, 'Nick Carleton is just a hunk.'

'He's an excellent actor, though,' Liz pointed out. 'You should have seen him in *The Summer House*. Even Mike thought it was good, and you know how critical he usually is.'

Sarah clasped her hands together ecstatically. 'I can't believe it—Nick Carleton in Stynch Magna! Wait till I tell Geoff! If he's here all summer, I'd be bound to meet him, wouldn't I?'

'You're welcome to him, Sarah.' Abby picked up her basket. 'Personally I intend to have as little to do with him as possible!'

CHAPTER TWO

THE shop door jangled behind Abby as she stepped out into the street, and she walked home slowly, thinking about the smug expression in Nick Carleton's eyes. She knew the other girls found her attitude strange; for them an American film star represented glamour and excitement, but for Abby Nick meant only a summer with a constant and vivid reminder of the bleak time in her life she had tried so hard to put behind her.

For the next two weeks, the village buzzed with excitement at the prospect of Nick Carleton's arrival, and Abby was soon heartily sick of hearing his name.

'I mean, what's so interesting about the wretched man, anyway?' she asked Liz, crossly plucking blades of grass from the lawn where they were lying enjoying another hot day.

Liz smiled tolerantly and stretched. 'He's rich, famous and—whatever you may say, Abby—very, ver-ry attractive. How much more interesting do you want?'

Abby had reluctantly waved Letty off to Australia, still serenely unaware of the celebrity of her tenant. She had been dreading Nick Carleton's arrival ever since, but a further week had passed with no sign of him.

It seemed typically irritating of him that he reappeared just when she was beginning to relax and

think that perhaps he had changed his mind after all.
She was watering the garden and chatting absently to
the plants, a habit she had picked up from Letty, when
the deep, American voice behind her made her spin
round, one hand to throat. Her heart began to thud,
slowly and almost painfully.

'Do you always talk to flowers?' Nick was watching
her over the gate. Without being invited, he vaulted
over it into her garden. 'How are you doing, Abigail?'

Abby had resented being able to remember his
features in such vivid detail, but she had forgotten the
subtle way he seemed to somehow dominate his surroundings. He exuded a zest and confidence which left
Abby feeling stupidly defensive, and, although she
tried to tell herself that his brightly striped jacket was
tasteless and clashed with his trousers, it didn't dimin-
ish the overwhelming impact of his presence.

Suddenly realising that she must look ridiculous
standing there holding a watering can in one hand, she
set it down and cleared her throat, saying the first
thing that came into her head. 'So you decided to
come after all.'

Nick grinned. 'Sure. Were you hoping I'd changed
my mind?'

'It had occurred to me.' Abby took refuge in her
haughty air.

'Tough luck, Abigail, I'm here for the duration.' He
had strolled over to join her, and, in an unthinking
attempt to put some space between her and his overwhelming personality, she took a step backwards,
horrified to find herself stumbling as she lost her
footing on the edge of the border.

She was saved by a strong hand which shot out and

closed round her elbow, setting her firmly back on the grass. 'Falling over herself to greet me,' he murmured, familiar laughter lurking in emerald eyes. His hand was hard against her skin and for a second his thumb stroked the soft inside of her elbow before Abby wrenched her arm away.

'No doubt that's what you expected!' she snapped, resisting the urge to touch her arm where it tingled still.

'Not from you, duchess, I have to admit.' Nick put his hands in the pockets of his trousers and stood looking at her thoughtfully. Her floaty, flowery dress in soft blues and greens seemed to blend into the border behind her, and as usual her hair was pinned up in a vaguely Edwardian style. 'Tell me,' he said, 'did your enquiries turn up anything suspect, or am I in the clear?'

'I found out that you're apparently a terribly famous film star or something, if that's what you wanted to know,' Abby replied, unable to keep the disparaging note from her voice.

He assumed a disappointed air. 'Is that all? I was hoping you'd at least be able to tell me the name of my mom's dog. I know lots about *you*.'

'I doubt that very much,' Abby said coldly.

'I know you're kind to rabbits and old ladies, but not to men. You're a beautiful girl, but you live alone. You don't like cars, but you'll talk to plants for some reason. You've been to the States, but you obviously don't like Americans much, so I figure you had a bad experience over there, and now you've buried yourself in the country to get over it. How am I doing?'

'Instant analysis—how typically American!' She

picked up the watering can again and turned back to the border. 'Unfortunately I'm not blessed with your amazing insight into people. You might have told me how well known you are—or did you have a good laugh at the thought of me trying to find out who you were?'

'Don't give me that, Abigail. What was I going to say? "I've been on the cover of *People*"?'

Abby looked blank. 'On the cover of what?'

'*People* magazine.' He rolled his eyes. 'No, I guess you wouldn't have come across it. It's a magazine full of gossip about people like me that you don't know and probably wouldn't want to—oh, it doesn't matter. You didn't even believe I was an actor. Would you have believed me if I'd started boasting about what a star I was?'

'Perhaps not.'

'Of *course* not! Anyway, it made a nice change to meet someone who didn't "love my show"—as you obviously don't.'

'Oh, I'm assured it's the best thing ever to come out of Hollywood,' said Abby, emptying the last of the water over the wilting stocks. 'Apart from your films, of course.'

'And you've no intention of ever watching any of them, right?'

'I don't have a television and I've better things to do than sit in a stuffy cinema watching rubbishy films. But don't worry, you'll find plenty of fans in Stynch Magna.'

'That's good,' he said, deadpan. 'I need lots of adoration to feed my huge ego.'

'I can well believe it,' Abby retorted acidly, knowing that he was teasing her, but unable to resist replying.

Nick laughed. Didn't he ever take anything seriously? He probably didn't believe that anyone could not be over the moon at the thought of meeting him. He was looking round the garden now, at the bright masses of different colours and shapes, from the tall delphiniums and hollyhocks, jaunty Michaelmas daisies and sweet-smelling lilac to the tiny alpines that spread in colourful mats along the edge of the path, tumbling in gay profusion over the stones. It was very quiet in this last flush of the day, and the air was heady with the mingled fragrance of the garden.

'It's beautiful here,' he said, and his gaze came back to Abby, framed by flowers, the golden evening light in her hair and the watering can clutched in front of her as if to ward off his magnetic charm 'Beautiful,' he repeated softly, his eyes on her face.

They stared at each other in a silence suddenly vibrant with awareness until Abby found her voice with an effort. 'Yes, it is.' She cleared her throat of the embarrassing huskiness. What was the matter with her? 'There isn't much to do around here though. You'll probably be very bored.'

'Oh, I don't think I'll be bored, Abigail,' Nick said. Green eyes smiled down into grey, and Abby couldn't have looked away if she had tried. 'I don't think I'll be bored at all.'

The first thing Abby saw when she drew back her curtains the next morning was the racing green of the Rolls-Royce, grand and gleaming on the grassy verge.

It reminded her all too vividly of her new neighbour.

Abby stared down at the car, still holding the curtain with one hand. Why, oh, why, had he had to come here? He was so like Stephen! Stephen hadn't had those film star looks, it was true, but he had had that same confidence in his own charm, the same smug humour, the same belief that he was God's gift to women. Abby had no intention of falling for it again.

Pushing Nick Carleton firmly out of her mind, she splashed cold water on her face, pulled on a pair of old shorts and a sleeveless T-shirt, and ran downstairs. He might be able to spend the summer 'getting away from it all', but she had work to do.

Abby never wore shoes if she could help it, and outside the grass was still cool and damp with dew beneath her feet. It was going to be another hot day. The studio shed stood at the bottom of the garden, and the familiar smell of methylated spirits and paint met her as she wedged open the studio door and slipped on the stained old shirt she used as an overall. Settling a large pair of horn-rimmed spectacles on her nose, she was ready for work.

Pictures lay stacked against the wall and the workbench was covered in an array of bottles and brushes. Methodically, Abby selected what she would need and laid the trolley next to the easel before sitting down and contemplating the canvas. She loved this moment, just before she started on a painting, wondering what she would find, and she flexed her fingers experimentally. The studio was filled with light from the large picture window which looked out over an uninterrupted view of rolling fields and woods, and Abby felt a surge of happiness as she picked up a brush and bent to work.

So absorbed was she that Nick Carleton was forgotten entirely until the unfamiliar blare of rock music from next door announced that the American was awake. Abby's head jerked up at the abrupt shattering of the silence.

'What the——?' Tutting impatiently, Abby turned back to the easel, but it was impossible to concentrate with that beat thumping away in the background. With growing resentment she glared at the picture in front of her. How could she be expected to work with that din going on?

At last the song came to an end, leaving the silence unnaturally loud. Abby just had time to breathe a sigh of relief before a strident chord announced another tune—if you could call it a tune! Snatching off her glasses, Abby stormed out of the studio and over to the gate dividing the two gardens.

'Turn that music off!' she shouted.

There was no response. He probably couldn't hear anything over the music, she thought furiously, and pushed open the gate. The kitchen door was wide open, so she stalked in without knocking.

She was momentarily disconcerted to find the kitchen empty, but the next instant Nick appeared in the doorway, rubbing wet hair with a towel. In confusion Abby realised that he was naked except for a brief towel wrapped around his waist. The broad shoulders seemed to fill the doorway and there were still droplets of water on his tanned skin. He was lean and hard, all tightly compacted strength, with not an ounce of superfluous flesh on him. The effect was overwhelming. Abby swallowed, hating her body for the way it seemed to tingle in instinctive response.

'Hi, there!'

Abby had the illogical conviction that he had deliberately taken off his clothes to distract her and she seized on the excuse for a rush of renewed anger. 'Turn that music down!'

Nick looked faintly surprised. 'Is it bothering you?'

'Of course it's bothering me! I wouldn't be here if it wasn't!' Abby's grey eyes were stormy, and he lifted one eyebrow, as if amused at her obvious indignation.

'What's the problem? Don't you like it?'

'It's far too loud—I can hardly hear myself think!'

With an insulting lack of concern, Nick finished towelling his hair and dabbed the water off his face before draping the towel round his shoulders and advancing into the kitchen. Abby wished he had stayed where he was; he seemed to loom over her in the small, low-ceilinged room.

'The music's not that loud,' he said at last. 'And you don't seem to be having any problems hearing me.'

Abby's lips tightened. 'It *is* Sunday,' she pointed out.

'So? What's Sunday got to do with it?'

'It's an unwritten rule here that you don't make a disturbance on a Sunday.' She folded her arms tightly in front of her in an unconscious gesture of defence against his overwhelming masculinity.

Nick was unperturbed. He opened the fridge and poured himself an orange juice. 'Sorry, lady,' he drawled, exaggerating his American accent. 'I guess I don't have a copy of the same rulebook. Where I come from, listening to some perfectly inoffensive music on a Sunday doesn't constitute a disturbance!'

'Well it's a pity you don't go back to where you

come from—where I come from, it does,' Abby
snapped. 'I'm trying to work. I can't possibly concentrate with all that noise going on. Couldn't you at least
turn it down?'

'I could, yes.' He looked down at her with a glint of
steel in his eyes. 'Couldn't you at least ask me nicely?'
His mimicry was uncomfortably recognisable, and
Abby flushed slightly. 'I thought you English were
supposed to be so hot on politeness,' he went on, 'or
is that just a quaint old tradition now?'

Through clenched teeth Abby said, 'Would you
please turn the music down?'

'Certainly.' With an exaggerated flourish, Nick
turned a dial on the huge cassette player perched on
top of the fridge and cut the music off in mid-chord.
'Is that better?'

'Thank you.' Abby was icily polite.

'Just trying to be a good neighbour.' He grinned at
her. 'Perhaps you could let me know when I *am*
allowed to listen to music? I'd hate to disturb your
routine. Let's see. . .you presumably work in the
mornings, you'll want to have your lunch in peace,
afternoons are out, I guess, so are evenings. . .maybe
I could have an hour about teatime?'

'That won't be necessary.' Abby turned to go, aware
that he was making fun of her. 'It's none of my
business what you do. You can hold wild orgies in here
for all I care—as long as I can't hear it.'

'Wouldn't be much of a wild orgy if you couldn't
hear it,' he pointed out.

'That's your problem,' she said stonily. 'Just keep it
to your side of the garden wall.'

'Yes, ma'am!' Nick saluted smartly. 'Message received and understood!'

His mocking laughter followed her as Abby marched back to the studio, venting her bad temper on a couple of inoffensive weeds en route, and wasted ten minutes banging around among her paints. He was unbearable! He was obviously quite incapable of taking anything seriously. The least he could have done was apologise for disturbing her, but, no! She was the one left feeling guilty for making him turn his music off.

Jamming her spectacles back on, she tried to settle back at her easel, but found it even harder to concentrate than before. The quiet was deafening and she was hideously aware of Nick waiting for her to finish before he switched the music on again.

The memory of his strong body shimmered before the painting. Strong and hard. What would it be like to touch? Abby tried to shake her thoughts free, but they circled inevitably back to tanned, tantalising skin and an impression of suppressed power.

In exasperation she got up again to fetch a sketch pad. She often found sketching a good way to clear her mind and now she let her pencil move almost of its own accord across the paper. When she had finished, Nick's darkly handsome features gazed back up at her.

Abby held the pad away from her, pleased. She had given him exactly the right smug expression! Quickly she sketched in his body with its skimpy towel covering and then on an impulse drew a caricature of herself shouting at him, seeing the funny side for the first time. What must he have thought of her, bursting into the cottage like that to drag him out of his bath?

With a chuckle she tossed the pad back on to the

bench and picked up her brush once more. Serve him right for playing that appalling music! At least she had made it clear that she wanted him to stay firmly on the other side of the garden wall.

Barely a minute later a fluttering movement caught her eye, and she looked up to see a large white handkerchief being waved slowly back and forth in the doorway by an unseen hand.

Shifting the spectacles down her nose, she gazed severely over the rim. 'Yes?' she said with an air of long suffering.

The handkerchief was whisked aside, and the next instant Nick materialised in the doorway. 'Could we call a truce while I come to ask a favour?' He had put on bright surfer-style shorts and a T-shirt proclaiming 'COME AND GET ME' in big letters.

Abby winced. 'What can I do for you?' she asked, deliberately unencouraging.

Undeterred, Nick took her words as an invitation and strolled over to where she sat by the easel. 'I didn't know you were an artist,' he said in surprise.

'Really? I thought you'd already found out everything there was to know about me,' replied Abby in dulcet tones.

'Oh, not *everything*. I think you merit closer study than that.' Nick's voice was bland, but his eyes danced, and, to her horror, Abby felt a blush steal up her neck. She turned hastily back to the easel.

'As it happens, I'm not an artist, much as I'd like to be. I merely clean and restore other artists' work.'

He was standing behind her now and looking over her shoulder at the Victorian landscape on the easel. The stains of age had almost completely obscured the original picture, but it was just possible to make out some figures in one corner, while Abby had started work on the shape of a house.

'Do you know what it is?' he asked.

'I'm not sure, but I have a feeling it might be a picture of Stynch Manor.' She felt twitchy with him standing so close to her and tensed to avoid flinching as he leant forward to peer more closely at the painting.

'Stynch Manor? Is that the big house round here?'

She nodded. 'I can't be sure yet until I've cleaned a bit more, but that wing there is set at an odd angle, just like the manor, and that tree looks familiar as well.' She was relieved when he moved away and hoisted himself on to the workbench.

'It must be quite a skilled job,' he commented. 'How long will it take you to finish a picture like that?'

'Two or three weeks, perhaps. This one is rather dirty, but the condition is not too bad.'

'Two or three weeks! You must be a very patient lady, Abigail Smith.' He watched the clean lines of her profile as she bent towards the canvas and with infinite care swabbed a small patch of paint. Her upper lip was caught between her teeth in concentration.

'Only in some things,' she said when she had finished, but her pointed comment was lost on Nick, who had jumped off the bench and was now inspecting the studio, looking through the paintings stacked against the wall, picking up paints, flourishing a large paintbrush. Couldn't he sit still for five minutes? Abby wished he would go. She couldn't concentrate with him prowling around like that.

'Hey! Did you do this?' With a sinking heart she

realised that he had found the sketch she had done of him.

'Obviously.' Who else did he think had done it?

'It's great!' He glanced over at her. 'Do I really look that pleased with myself to you?'

'Since you ask—yes,' Abby said cuttingly, as she continued to work on the painting.

Nick grimaced at the sketch, then tapped a finger against the caricature she had done of herself looking ferocious, hands on hips, in mid-nag. 'You know, you didn't quite get your own expression right, Abigail. You looked much more terrifying than that. You should have drawn me cowering behind the kitchen table!'

When Abby refused to rise to the bait and merely sent him a look over the rim of her glasses, he went on, 'Seriously, it's a brilliant drawing. I thought you said you weren't an artist.'

'I'm not. I enjoy sketching, but I know my own limitations. I could never make a living as an artist.'

'And do you make a living out of doing this— restoration, did you say?' Nick replaced a paint pot and unscrewed the top of another bottle, wrinkling his nose at the pungent smell.

Abby shrugged. 'Of sorts. Enough to get by, anyway. I certainly can't afford any of the luxuries people like you seem to consider so essential, but I'm quite happy with what I've got.'

'I'd be interested to hear what you think my essentials are.' Nick folded his arms and leant casually against the wall. 'Well? Go on.'

Abby selected another brush from the trolley with

care. 'I don't know. . .car, television, washing-machine—that kind of thing,' she said, a touch of irritation in her voice.

Nick threw back his head and laughed, a deeply attractive masculine laugh. 'I think you'd find that the luxuries of Hollywood have moved beyond washing-machines and televisions!'

'That's exactly my point.' Abby frowned at the canvas. 'I'm not entirely naïve, you know. All I'm saying is that the things you take for granted are luxuries as far as I'm concerned.'

He seemed to consider this. 'Maybe I do take those things for granted, but it doesn't mean that I think they're essential. Hell, I'm looking forward to a summer without a jacuzzi!'

Abby ignored his grin. 'What on earth are you going to do with yourself?' she asked. 'There's nothing here for someone like you.'

'Someone like me?' Nick lifted an eyebrow. 'What's that supposed to mean? Someone American?'

'I thought you all had to be constant achievers and fill your time *meaningfully*,' she said scornfully. She was ruffled by his questioning, unsettled by his near-ness, and in defence fought back with old prejudices.

'Don't you think that's something of a massive over-generalisation?'

'Not in my experience.' Abby clamped her mouth shut.

'Boy, you sure are prejudiced against Americans, aren't you, Abigail Smith? All two hundred and fifty million of us! I guess it's useless to tell you that we're not all alike?' He looked at Abby hopefully, but sighed when her expression remained mutinous. 'What happened to you in Washington to make you dislike us all so much?'

Abby didn't want to talk to Nick about what had happened. She put down her brush with a click. 'Did you want something?' she reminded him with frigid politeness.

'Oh, yes.' Nick slapped his forehead, diverted. 'I know it sounds a horrible cliché, but do you have any coffee? I clean forgot the shops are closed on a Sunday here. I hate to bother you, but I'm finding it kind of hard to face a Sunday morning without a shot of caffeine.'

What could she say? Pushing her glasses on top of her head, Abby stood up. Nick eyed her long, slim legs appreciatively.

'I only have instant, I'm afraid,' she said, determined not to let him rile her any more. 'Will that do?'

'Sure. I'm not proud.'

Abby glanced at him sharply. Was it her imagination, or had he stressed the 'I' in there?

'How's Peter?' Nick asked as they walked back to the cottage.

'Peter?' Abby was taken unawares by his sudden question.

'Your boyfriend. What did Letty call him? Your young man?'

'Peter is not my boyfriend or my young man!' Abby gritted her teeth. No matter how many times she denied it, nobody ever seemed to believe her, least of all Peter Middleton and Letty Walker!

'That's good. Then he won't object if I ask you out

on a date. I'd like to see the country round here and it would be nice to have a guide. Will you come?'

They had reached the kitchen and Abby was glad of the excuse to search for a jam jar while she gave herself time to think. He was an attractive man. There was no real reason not to bury her prejudices for once and enjoy an innocent day out. And yet. . .

Abby hesitated, aware that innocent was not a word that sat easily with Nick Carleton. She was conscious of a tingling undercurrent of danger in her physical awareness of him that raised her defences in alarm and left her resenting the way he was disturbing her nice, peaceful, safe existence. She had fallen for it before, and she didn't want to go through it again. Easier by far to remember her prejudices and keep reminding herself that he was American. She didn't want to go through falling for one of them again either.

'You don't look very keen,' Nick said, looking round the cosy kitchen with frank interest. 'What's the matter?'

Abby got the coffee out of the cupboard and turned to face him squarely. 'Why me?' she asked bluntly. 'You already know I don't like Americans. I haven't been particularly nice to you. There must be any number of people in the village who'd love to show you round.'

'I haven't met them yet,' Nick said reasonably. 'I've only met you, and you. . .well, let's say you intrigue me.' He grinned. 'Maybe I'd like to change your mind about Americans.'

At that moment, alerted by sounds of activity in the kitchen, Elijah appeared in the doorway with a studied yawn. He stopped at the sight of a strange man with his mistress and regarded Nick with unblinking yellow eyes.

'Elijah,' Abby answered Nick's enquiring look, adding as he crouched down, 'I'm afraid he's not very friendly with strangers.'

'Like his mistress, huh?' Nick's voice was teasing, and to her chagrin the tabby went straight up to him and rubbed himself against his knee. She bit her lip, but when Nick shot a glinting glance up at her she was unable to resist smiling back.

'He did that deliberately!' she accused.

'I know. Typical of a cat.' Nick gave Elijah a final scratch behind his ear and stood up. 'They're beautiful creatures, aren't they? So elegant and independent.' His eyes, warm and disturbing, rested on her face as he spoke.

'I'll get you the coffee,' she said hurriedly, and began spooning coffee into the jam jar.

'You haven't said whether we've got a date yet,' he reminded her.

Abby concentrated on screwing on the top of the jam jar. The chestnut tints in her hair were very pronounced in the sunlight streaming through the kitchen door and loose tendrils were escaping from the combs she had used to pin it away from her face.

'I'm rather busy at the moment,' she said eventually, unable to think of a better excuse.

'That's OK. Whenever you're free.' Nick was obviously amused at her reluctance. 'I've never had this trouble persuading a girl to go out on a date before.'

'You surprise me,' Abby said frostily.

'Now I suppose you think I'm conceited, as well as

being American!' He heaved an exaggerated sigh. 'I can see I'm going to have to work hard to impress you.'

'Please don't bother.' She thrust the jar of coffee at him. 'Here's your coffee. Now, if you don't mind. . .'

Nick tossed the jar in the air. 'Sure, I'll let you get back to work. Thanks for the coffee. And don't forget our date!' Whistling, he vaulted over the gate.

'We haven't got a date!' Abby shouted after him, but he was gone.

Much to Abby's disgust, but not really to her surprise, the village soon took Nick to its heart, and it seemed as if she couldn't go anywhere without having to listen to eulogies about her famous neighbour.

'So friendly and natural,' they gushed in the village shop.

'Always a nice word for everybody,' they agreed in the pub, and even Ted Butler, the butcher and a man not noted for love of his fellow men, grunted that he seemed a sensible enough bloke.

Praise indeed, thought Abby wryly, picking up her lamb chop. None of them had to live next door to Nick Carleton though! She found his presence increasingly exasperating, but, if pushed to explain exactly what she objected to, could only protest feebly that he was 'always there'. There was always music spilling out of the windows—a bewildering variety from heavy rock to classical—but she couldn't, in all honesty, complain of it being too loud.

And it wasn't as if he interrupted her. He always kept strictly to his side of the garden wall. Abby knew it was unfair to grumble about a man who sat in the garden and read quietly; it was just that he always gave the impression of being on the point of leaping into action which she found downright unsettling. She wished she wasn't so *aware* of him the whole time, and began to hope he would do something—anything!—to justify her growing irritation other than his predilection for what, in her opinion anyway, were horribly garish shirts, but which everyone else seemed to admire.

'You think anything other than brown or grey is garish,' Liz pointed out, and refused to agree that Nick looked anything like a stereotype.

There had been no more mention of their 'date'. If Nick saw her in the garden, he would look up and flash that smile with its lurking laughter, and Abby would respond with a cool nod, but it seemed as if he had decided to ignore her in favour of the more congenial companionship he found in the village. Well, good, that was just the way she wanted it!

CHAPTER THREE

THE gate at the far end of the garden opened on to a dusty track, which ran between scraggy hedgerows down to a small stream, running sluggishly now after weeks without rain. Abby had fallen into the habit of walking down barefoot every evening after watering the garden, Elijah pacing sedately beside her.

This daily ritual was marred only by the deep cattlegrid which marked the boundary of the meadow. To Abby, this grid seemed to have been positioned deliberately between her and the stream. As a child she had been terrified of grids; a long-forgotten story had convinced her that something dank and horrible lurked down there, waiting for a small foot to slip through the bars. She could remember making a horrible fuss and insisting that her father carried her across. Even now, as she edged over the grid, the memory of his strong, reassuring arms would come flooding back.

Of course, Abby reminded herself, she was a grown woman now. Of course there was nothing beneath the grid. Vaguely ashamed of such a ridiculously childish fear, she would still check that nothing hid below before crossing as near to the edge as possible with a fine display of nonchalance.

On that particular evening, Abby bestowed a frigid nod on Nick Carleton before unlatching the garden gate and making her way along the track. The dust was warm and gritty between her toes, reminding her of countless childhood expeditions. As always, she hesitated by the grid and peered cautiously down into its depths, recoiling with an involuntary gasp as she realised that for once there was indeed something down there!

The grid was seething with small brown frogs. Abby grimaced with distaste and was about to cross over when something made her stop and look again. On closer inspection she could see that the frogs were piled on top of each other, most squatting motionless while a few more determined individuals took futile leaps at the wall in an effort to get out.

Abby bit her lip. They were obviously trapped, and would equally obviously die if she left them there. She didn't fancy spending the rest of the summer stepping over hundreds of little corpses every time she went for a walk.

Resigned, she knelt down and wriggled her arm through the bars of the grid. Frogs, of all the revolting things!

Her hand dangled uselessly above the frogs, so she shifted position until she lay flat on her stomach, one cheek in the dust and her arm stretched to its limit. Screwing up her face for a final effort, she stretched one more time as a familiar American voice above her enquired with some amusement, 'Lost something?'

Antipathy forgotten in her preoccupation, Abby merely grunted, intent on pushing her arm just a bit further through the bars. 'No. . .ah! No, it's useless.' She withdrew her arm and sat up. It was red and sore where she had scraped it against the metal and she rubbed it gingerly.

Nick squatted down beside her. 'What are you trying to do down there?'

'See for yourself.'

He followed her pointing finger and whistled when he saw the heaving mass of trapped frogs. 'What are they all doing down there?'

'Trying to get out. They're trapped.' Abby had recovered her breath a bit, and sat back on her heels. Her cloud of chestnut-brown hair had escaped from the combs and she pushed it out of the way, rubbing her grubby face absently. 'I think they were probably trying to get to the stream. It's been so dry there's hardly any moisture around for them. They could have fallen in, or maybe jumped in because it looked cool and shady, but now they're stuck. It's just as dry down there now.'

There was a curious expression in Nick's eyes as he turned to look at her, and she was suddenly acutely aware of what a mess she must look, with her grimy face, dusty dress and hair all anyhow. Instinctively, she raised a hand to wipe her cheek where it had lain in the dust.

'What were you planning to do with them if you reached them?' Nick appeared not to have noticed her momentary confusion and was peering down into the grid.

'Er—well, I don't know really. Lift them out, I suppose.'

'What, all of them? There are hundreds of them down there!'

'I haven't had time to do a feasibility study yet,' Abby snapped, with a return to her old form.

Nick ignored her, and tried wriggling his own arm

through the bars. It stuck just below the elbow. 'What we need are some tongs or something. Got any barbecue tongs?'

'That's a good idea.' Abby stared at him in reluctant admiration, wishing she had thought of it herself.

'I'm not just a pretty face,' he said modestly. 'I reckon we need to make some kind of ramp for them too. I don't fancy spending all night down here.'

'Could you?' Abby looked doubtful.

'Sure. Being a film star doesn't mean you can't knock up a shelf as well as the next man—or woman,' he added, with a look at Abby's face.

She laughed and relented. 'To tell you the truth, I'm hopeless at that sort of thing. Could you really make a ramp for them?'

'Easy.' Nick got to his feet and began brushing the dust off his pale cotton trousers. 'I used to make all sorts of things when I was a kid. All I need is a bit of wood and a few nails.'

'I expect I can find you those.' Abby made as if to get up too and Nick put out a hand to haul her to her feet. His fingers were very strong and warm against hers. Quickly she pulled her hand away and made a great show of dusting herself down as well.

'I'll get a watering can. Maybe some of them will revive if I moisten them.'

'What are you, some kind of frogophile?' Nick asked as they walked back along the track.

'Ugh, no. I think they're revolting things.'

'You seem to be going to a lot of trouble for them,' he commented.

Abby shot him a defiant look. 'So are you.' Grey

eyes met green, and then they both chuckled. 'We can't just leave them to die,' she added feebly.

'No, I guess we can't.'

Nick's ramp was a great success. Wedging the narrow planks through the bars, they began prodding the more active frogs towards the sloping exit with a pair of barbecue tongs they had found in the Walkers' garden shed and the blunt end of Abby's kebab sticks.

'Stupid things,' she grumbled as the frogs jumped everywhere except on to the plank. 'Anyone would think they didn't want to escape.'

'Don't worry, this little fella's getting the idea.' With agonised concentration they watched as the frog slowly and reluctantly shuffled up the plank. Together they shared a whoop of triumph as Abby plucked him free of the bars and deposited him in a bucket.

'Yuk!' She wriggled her fingers in distaste. 'I hate the feel of them.'

It seemed entirely natural to be kneeling there with Nick, their hands touching as they poked and prodded the frogs up the ramp. Even so, Abby was very conscious of him beside her, of the hard line of his body and the vivid green of his eyes as he turned to smile at her. She found that she wasn't noticing his accent any more as he made her laugh with his characterisations of the little creatures. After a while they began to distinguish different personalities: the keen ones, the apathetic ones, those who hopped up in a businesslike way and those who fell off clumsily just as they neared the top. Nick did a different voice for each one brilliantly, and Abby giggled so helplessly she had to stop and wipe her eyes.

'I never thought I'd have so much fun with frogs!'

Nick looked at her slyly. 'Maybe you'll change your mind about Americans too,' he suggested, and Abby bit her lip, at a loss for a quick answer.

Together they carried the bucket full of the most deserving cases across the meadow and down to the stream. The sky was a deep lavender colour and beneath their feet the grass was cool and soft.

Gently Nick tipped the frogs out of the bucket at the water's edge and they watched them blink dopily at their new surroundings before hopping off one by one.

'Not so much as a thank-you,' Nick said in mock reproach.

Abby smiled at him through the dusk. 'Thank you,' she said simply.

'Hell, *you* don't need to thank me. I didn't do anything.'

'Yes, you did.' Abby sat down on an old log which lay half in, half out of the water. 'I'd never have got anywhere by myself.'

Nick sat down beside her and leant forward, resting his elbows on his knees. 'Most girls wouldn't have gone to all that trouble for a few frogs. Kittens, maybe, but not frogs.'

A lone frog crouched, half hidden, in the grass, and Abby's eyes rested on it thoughtfully. 'I think it was the thought of them being trapped in the grid. If it had been anywhere else I probably would have left them to get on with it.'

'What's so special about the grid?'

'It's always been my secret fear.' She gave an embarrassed shrug. 'When I was a little girl I used to

dream about slipping between the bars—a hand grab-
bing my ankle and pulling me down.' She stopped as
she saw Nick suppress a smile. 'Of course, I suppose
you never had an illogical fear!'

He was laughing openly now. 'I guess I just lacked
imagination as a kid. The only thing I was afraid of
was a walloping from my dad.' He paused, and the
laughter faded from his face. Without warning he
reached out to take her hand. 'Someone hurt you real
bad in the States, didn't they, Abby?'

Abby was shaken by his abrupt question, more so
by the effect of his touch, warm and comforting. He
had nice hands with long, blunt-ended fingers and
well-kept nails. Her own fingers ached to curl themselves round his, but she forced herself to let her hand
lie still within his grasp. 'What makes you say that?'
She hardly recognised her high, uncertain voice.

'It's obvious. You're pretty bitter about something
that happened to you there. People don't usually get
bitter unless they've been hurt.'

How could she explain about Stephen to someone
like Nick? Would he understand how Stephen had
dazzled her with his charm and confidence, how he
had taught her to trust and to love, how he had taught
her that trust and love were worthless things and easily
tossed aside? Nick was the same kind of man. . .wasn't
he? Except that Stephen would have had no time to
waste talking to people in the village who wouldn't be
useful to his career, and he certainly wouldn't have
been bothered with a few frogs.

Her hand felt safe and secure within his strong,
reassuring clasp. She was sure she could feel every
whorl on his fingertips. Abby moistened her lips,

forced her mind back to his question. 'I was unlucky, I suppose. I learnt a lesson more painfully than perhaps I need have done, that's all.' That's all? Well, it was enough for Nick Carleton.

'It was some guy who hurt you, wasn't it?' Nick's voice had an undercurrent in it that Abby didn't recognise.

'Isn't it always?' Abby forced a bright smile. 'I'm afraid it wasn't a very original storyline!'

'Sounds like one of my movies!' To her relief, Nick sensed that she didn't want to talk about it any more. He let go of her hand and changed the mood with an anecdote about a tediously unimaginative film he'd had a small role in at the beginning of his career. 'I thought it was great at the time. I really thought I'd hit the big time!'

'And now you really have,' said Abby, trying not to think of how cold and lost her hand felt.

Nick turned to look at her, and for once his eyes were thoughtful, even serious, as they took in the vulnerable grey eyes, the fine, sensitive face and the stubbornly proud set of her head. 'Yes,' he said slowly, 'I guess I have.'

They sat on in silence until at last the midges drove them away from the trees. In the last glimmering light they made their way back across the meadow, Nick with his hands thrust into his pockets, Abby lightly clasping her folded arms. She wished she could forget the touch of his hand. Stealing a sidelong glance at him, she found him watching her and they smiled wordlessly, almost shyly at each other. Abby felt an alarming glow settle somewhere deep inside her and she turned away hastily.

At the gate Nick paused with one hand on the latch, barring her way. 'Abigail?'

They were standing very close. Abby felt as if the breath were leaking out of her. Her heart seemed to pause, then its steady thud slowed until it was almost imperceptible.

'Yes?' Her voice was hardly more than a whisper.

Nick looked down at her while the silence burned between them. Abby longed for him to touch her again, dreaded her response. She dared not shatter her self-control by moving or breathing or speaking.

Perhaps her vulnerability showed in her face, for when he did reach out it was only to lay the back of his hand very gently against her cheek before he stood back from the gate.

'Goodnight.' His voice was so deep that it was almost inaudible, but it was enough to bring Abby back to reality. Bitter disappointment warred with relief as she muttered a brief goodnight in return and fled to the beckoning safety of her cottage.

Quarter past three. Abby frowned down at her watch and wished, not for the first time, that she could afford to buy a car. There were hours to wait before the bus back to Stynch Magna and her arms were aching from carrying heavy carrier-bags around the town. For once it was cloudy, but if anything the air felt hotter and more humid. Abby blew the hair out of her eyes as she flexed her fingers and bent to pick up the bags once more.

It was too stuffy to go to the library as she often did, and she couldn't face another shop. It looked as if it would have to be Horton's Teashop, she decided reluctantly. She supposed she could spin out a pot of weak tea and a stale scone for a while. The thought was unappealing. Why, oh, why, weren't there more buses? It was the only drawback to living in a rural area. Abby had come to dread her monthly sortie to Turlbury to stock up on the essentials she couldn't buy at the village shop. She always seemed to spend half the day trailing around the streets waiting for the bus home.

Dispiritedly, she began to cross the wide street towards the tea-shop when her eye was caught by a familiar name emblazoned above the cinema.

NICK CARLETON

Abby stared, her heart giving an odd thump of recognition. It was one thing to be told that Nick was famous, quite another to see it for herself. Almost of her own volition, her feet took her to stand outside the cinema where the still photographs were displayed. It was Nick all right. Nearly every shot featured his dark, piratical looks: rolling out of a car, suave in a dinner jacket, pinning a glamorous blonde to a pillow. Could this really be the same man who had helped her to rescue a few frogs?

Abby's eyes slid down the programme times. Next showing three-thirty. . .

Not that she had any intention of seeing the film! Turning away abruptly, she trudged down the street towards Horton's, her mind still on Nick. It was an odd feeling to see him at once so familiar and such a stranger. Which was the real Nick Carleton? The sophisticated film star or the casual neighbour who, despite his aggravating habits and the fact that he was undeniably American, she had unaccountably got used to having around?

Abby's mind veered quickly away from the memory of the previous evening. She cringed to remember how she had stood gazing up at him like one of his lovesick fans, her blood pounding at his nearness. She must have been bewitched by the soft summer evening light. She certainly didn't like the man, she was just. . .getting used to him. That was all.

Outside Horton's she hesitated, chewing her lip indecisively. What *would* it be like to see him on screen? If Horton's was packed, as it often was at this time, she might be forced to go to the cinema just to find somewhere to sit down. Abby allowed the thought to float past before brushing it aside and pushing open the door of the tea-room with unnecessary force.

There were plenty of free tables. Abby promptly left to retrace her steps to the cinema where she found herself staring at the programme times once more. Three-thirty. It was only just past that now.

A couple passed her and went inside and instinctively she glanced over her shoulder. After all she had had to say about the cinema, and Nick Carleton's films in particular, the last thing she wanted was for anyone to think she was even contemplating going to see one. But there were no familiar faces in Broad Street that afternoon.

She would go and have that tea. Picking up her bags once more, she took a few steps, wavered, put the bags down again, half lifted and immediately lowered them to the ground again. 'Oh, for heaven's sake!' she said impatiently, seizing her shopping and marching into the cinema before she had time to change her mind.

She emerged two hours later to stand blinking in the daylight. The bustling normality of Turlbury seemed incongruous after the film's exciting climax in Rio and Abby felt oddly disorientated. It had been so long since she had seen a film that she had forgotten the impact of the big screen. And Nick Carleton's presence had dominated the film to such an extent that Abby felt as if she had been pinned into her seat by the sheer force of his personality. There had been no trace of her irrepressible neighbour on screen. So absorbed had she been that she had forgotten Nick, forgotten Stynch Magna, forgotten everything except the heart-stopping excitement of the story.

Now she stood on the steps of the cinema, shaking her head as if to clear it. A car hooted near by, but Abby did not even hear as she picked up her bags and began to walk slowly down Broad Street. There was still plenty of time before the bus left.

It was an unexciting prospect. For the first time in years, Abby found herself longing for a little more excitement. *Was* she too young to bury herself in this quiet life of weekly shops and village gossip? Suddenly it all seemed just a little dull.

The blast of a car horn beside her jerked her out of her thoughts.

'Abigail! Abigail Smith!'

Abby looked round, confused.

'Over here!' It was Nick Carleton, leaning non-chalantly out of his green Rolls-Royce, one hand resting lightly on the steering-wheel, the other beck-oning. In a scarlet polo shirt which emphasised his dark features, it was as if he had stepped right out of the screen and Abby wondered for a moment if she was imagining things. The Rolls looked utterly out of place amid the sensible hatchbacks and estate cars of Turlbury and Nick looked equally exotic.

Feeling more disorientated than ever at this bizarre confusion of film and reality, Abby was incapable of doing more than putting down her shopping and waiting to see if things returned to normal.

With superb indifference to the double yellow lines, Nick slid the powerful car to the kerb, switched off the engine and stepped out.

'You can't stop there. That's a double yellow line.' Unable to fully grasp the situation, Abby found it easier to concentrate instead on a minor detail.

'That's very public-spirited of you, Abigail,' Nick approved, 'but I'm not going to be long. I was only going to offer you a lift. Where are you going?'

'Home,' said Abby hurriedly. 'I'm fine, thanks. Please don't bother.'

'No bother. I'm on my way home too.'

Out of the corner of her eye, Abby could see the disapproving stares of the passing motorists who were having to pull out past the Rolls. A traffic warden approached purposefully.

'Please, I——'

'Is this your car, sir?' The traffic warden was a solid, no-nonsense-looking woman in her forties, but she thawed visibly as Nick gave her the benefit of his dazzling smile.

'It is, and I know I shouldn't have stopped here, officer, but I just couldn't drive past Abigail here with all those bags.'

It was revolting, Abby thought, watching them indignantly, the way he had the woman eating out of his hand. Now he was even autographing her fine-book for her! That breezy charm and confidence reminded her bitterly of Stephen. How easily men like that sailed through life! Her memories of Stephen suddenly raw, Abby made to turn away, but Nick was too quick for her.

'We'd better move on before you fine us, officer!' Having reduced the traffic warden to smiles and blushes, Nick seized Abby's bags and tossed them into the back seat. 'Come on, Abigail, jump in!'

'Now, look, I don't really want——'

The next instant Abby felt herself swept off her feet into strong arms as Nick lifted her over the open top of the car and deposited her unceremoniously in the passenger seat. With a last disarming smile at the traffic warden, who was eyeing Abby enviously, he leapt lightly in beside her, put the car into gear and drove off before Abby had time to recover her breath.

CHAPTER FOUR

SCARLET with embarrassment, Abby turned on him. 'Was it really necessary to manhandle me like that?'

'You were holding up the traffic,' he said blandly, his eyes on the road ahead.

'Me? It wasn't me who parked on the double yellow lines! I suppose it's too much to hope that that traffic warden gave you a ticket?'

'I hate to disappoint you, but apparently she's one of my greatest fans.'

'I don't suppose you ever get a fine,' Abby said sulkily as they stopped at a red light. A group of girls on the pavement were pointing at the car and waving excitedly at Nick, who smiled and waved back.

'It's one of the advantages of being famous,' he agreed, easing the car away from the lights.

Abby sniffed and turned her head away.

'Oh, come on, you're not really angry with me, are you, Abigail Smith?'

'Don't call me that!' she said crossly. 'I've got the point that you can remember my name. Why can't you just call me Abby like everyone else?'

'Abby-like-everyone-else sounds a bit of a mouthful to me.' Nick grinned, adding, as he encountered a speaking look from Abby, 'Sorry, I always did like to play it for cheap laughs!'

'Obviously!'

'Anyway,' he went on, 'I like Abigail Smith. It's cool and English and old-fashioned, like you.'

'I am *not* old-fashioned,' Abby said through clenched teeth.

'You aren't? A beautiful girl like you, living alone in a cottage with just a cat and garden—isn't that just a little bit old-fashioned? And why do you always tie your hair up like that?' He looked moodily at the mass of chestnut hair pinned on top of her head. 'Why don't you ever let it down?'

'It's cooler like this,' Abby said defensively, resisting the urge to touch it.

Nick's eyes flickered over her face. 'If you say so.' His voice was half baffled, half amused, and Abby shot him a resentful glance. They were just coming to the edge of the town and the road stretched empty before them. Nick put his foot down on the accelerator and the big car surged forward, pressing Abby back into the soft leather seat.

'How did you like the movie?' he asked abruptly.

'What?' Abby was caught unawares, and Nick's green eyes mocked her gently.

'Don't try and deny it, Abigail. I saw you coming out of the cinema. Perhaps I should say, how did you enjoy the *film*?'

Of course, Nick *would* have to be the one person to see her! Abby suppressed a wince as she remembered all she had had to say on the subject. It was too much to hope that he had forgotten. 'It was all right,' she said grudgingly.

'I thought you didn't like movies,' Nick said with another of his disconcerting, glinting glances.

'I don't. It was a choice between a film or two hours

in Horton's Teashop. If you'd ever been to Horton's, you'd know that it wasn't much of a recommendation to choose the film.' Abby's voice was crisp, and Nick threw back his head and laughed.

'Fair enough. Well, tell me honestly, Abby, what you thought of it. You won't hurt my feelings.'

'I wasn't worried about that!' snapped Abby.

'No, I guess, you weren't. Go on, I'd like to know what you thought.'

Abby shrugged. 'I thought the plot was pretty silly, but it was so exciting it didn't really matter. I mean, at the time it doesn't matter, but if you think about it, those situations are all so unrealistic. And if I'd been chased all over South America, I certainly wouldn't look as immaculate as Charlotte Canning did at the end of it all.'

'No,' Nick said thoughtfully. 'You're a different type from Charlotte.' His smile was warm. 'Go on.'

She hesitated. She was very conscious of him beside her, of the strong hands holding the powerful car with ease. A wave of heat swept over her without warning as she remembered those same hands making love to Charlotte Canning on screen. It had not even been a very explicit love scene, but, still, Abby had found it uncomfortably erotic and she wished she could banish the memory of it from her mind.

'What about the ending?' Nick prompted.

'The ending?' With difficulty, Abby wrenched her mind back to the conversation. 'I think the heroine would have done better to have stayed at home and married the policeman.'

'Security being more important than passion? Yes, I

suppose you would think that. But why opt for second best?'

'It might be best in the long run.'

Nick's eyes rested on her averted profile, but he made no comment and they drove on in silence. The sun had broken through the clouds and the dappled light through the trees flickered on the long bonnet as they sped along the narrow lanes. The wind caught at Abby's hair and teased long tendrils away from her face. Despite herself, she felt her antagonism dissolve in the sheer enjoyment of sun and speed and the all-enveloping luxury of the Rolls. It really was a beautiful car!

Once she turned her head and found Nick watching her with a smile and spontaneously she smiled back. Surprise and something else flared in his eyes before he had to turn his attention back to the road. Inexplicably, Abby felt the blood begin to sing in her veins and, although she turned her face towards the hedgerows rushing past, the look in Nick's eyes danced before her own, and her mind lingered on the way his brown hand rested surely on the gear stick as he changed down to round a sharp bend.

Never had the fifteen-mile drive passed so quickly. All too soon the car was slowing down and sliding at a sedate pace through the village. Abby caught a glimpse of Sarah's interested face as they passed the shop and, recalled to a sense of her surroundings, she sat up straighter.

'You've missed the turning.'

'I know. Remember that guided tour you promised me? I thought we could start with the church.'

'You did, did you?' Abby was annoyed by his easy

assumption that she would fall in with his plans. 'I don't remember making any such promise. And what if I happen to be busy this afternoon?'

'So busy you spend two hours watching a movie?' Nick asked slyly.

'Only because I was waiting for the bus,' she began, but a smile trembled on her lips at his understanding grin, and she capitulated without further protest. 'It's just up here on the right.'

The church was set back from the road, half hidden by a row of old yew trees.

'To keep the witches away,' Abby explained, plucking a leaf as they ducked beneath a gnarled branch which hung over the path.

'No kidding?' Nick looked around the churchyard with interest. The older gravestones leant at different angles, many so covered with moss they were impossible to read, while others brooded, forgotten, in the deep shade of the yews. 'It's a pretty spooky place, isn't it? I guess I might believe in witches too, if I were here on a dark night.'

'I don't find it at all spooky,' said Abby. 'I like to think how long this church has been here at the centre of the village. Just imagine how many people have stood right here over the years.' Automatically, they both looked down at their feet.

Nick laughed. 'Quite a few, right? How old is the church?'

Abby pursed her lips and surveyed the effortlessly graceful lines of the church, while Nick watched the small crease of concentration between her brows. 'I don't know exactly,' she said. 'The transept is supposed to be Norman, but I think most of it dates from the fourteenth century. I should say it's about six or seven hundred years old.'

He whistled, impressed. 'Seven hundred years! You sound so blasé about it.'

'I'm not really. I love the sense of history you get in England.'

'Mmm.' He gave her a sidelong glance. 'As long as you don't live in the past the whole time. The present has plenty to offer too, Abigail.'

'Shall we go inside?' Abby's voice was cold. She had no desire to get into another discussion of how old-fashioned she was. 'You're the one who wanted to see the church.'

Together they pulled open the heavy oak door and stepped inside. Sunlight through the stained glass windows threw soft puddles of colour on to the worn flagstones and it was very quiet except for the sound of their footsteps. Nick prowled around, inspecting every nook and cranny, and deciphering the wall plaques, while Abby rather absently removed the dead heads from the flower arrangements.

'It's a beautiful church,' Nick said, coming to join her in the aisle. 'It makes you feel pretty unimportant, doesn't it?'

Walking slowly down the aisle, Abby reflected that Nick was a constant surprise to her. He had seemed so irritatingly frivolous and happy-go-lucky at first, not at all the kind of man who would appreciate the hushed beauty of an old church.

She ran her fingers along the edge of a pew, black and shiny with age, and wrinkled her nose at the mustiness of the air.

'They need to do so much work in here. It's terrible

to think that if they can't find the money, this church will just crumble away.'

Nick glanced around him. 'It seems OK to me.'

'Well, it isn't.' Abby frowned at his easy optimism. 'You only have to smell the air to realise how rotten everything is.'

'And are you just going to wring your hands, or is someone going to do something about it?' For once Nick seemed really angry. He sat on a pew, then immediately leapt up and began striding up and down the nave, radiating energy. The sheer vigour of the man seemed indecently earthy for the timeless peace of the church, and Abby bristled.

'We don't need you to tell us how to look after our church,' she snapped. 'Someone *is* doing something. But it takes time to raise enough money. We're not all swimming in it, like in the States.'

'In the States we go out and work for what we need. We don't sit around and complain about how poor we are!' Nick flashed back, then restrained his temper with a visible effort. 'What is being done, then?' He sounded brisk and efficient, which annoyed Abby even more.

'Coffee mornings, jumble sales, you know the kind of thing.' At Nick's incredulous expression she added defensively, 'And the church fête usually brings in quite a bit of money.'

He followed her to the door, shaking his head. 'The church fête! Boy, this really is village England!'

Abby stalked out into the churchyard. 'You know where to go if you don't like it!'

'Hey!' Nick grasped her wrist and pulled her round to face him. 'Hey!' he said again, shaking her gently as he stared down into her stormy grey eyes. 'I do like it here, I like it here very much. You know I do. You're so damned touchy! I was only concerned that not enough was being done to save that beautiful building. I'm sorry if I sounded brash. OK?'

Refusing to meet his eyes, Abby nodded. She wished he would let go of her wrist. He was too overpowering at close quarters.

'And there's another thing,' he said softly.

'What?' she muttered.

His voice dropped even lower and he lifted her chin with one finger. 'You look beautiful when you're angry!'

Startled, Abby's eyes flew up to meet his, but, seeing the teasing laughter there, she wrenched herself away in sudden fury. 'Don't be so childish!' How dared he laugh at her? For a dizzying moment she had wondered if he was going to bend his head, pull her closer, gather her into his kiss. . .But his obvious amusement had jerked her back to cold reality. He was just playing with her, and the humiliation of knowing how near she had been to falling into his arms sharpened her anger and helped her ruthlessly suppress a bitter pang of disappointment.

Nick had ducked away under the yew trees, oblivious to the tumult of Abby's conflicting emotions, and was peering at the gravestones there. 'Look how old this one is! 1747. . .' He traced the lettering lightly with his fingers. 'Elizabeth, beloved wife of Jacob Smith. Relations of yours?'

'I doubt it. Smith is a very common name.' But it was impossible to stay cross with him for long. His enthusiasm was infectious and Abby found herself crouching next to him in the green shade as they deciphered the names. They spent almost an hour in the graveyard while Nick searched in vain for a Carleton and Abby tried not to think about how much she was enjoying his company.

It was only a short distance back to the cottages. Nick switched the engine off and turned towards her, one arm along the back of the seat, his hand close enough to touch her. Abby sat very still. She was trying desperately to look casual and as if her attention was riveted by the gleaming wooden dashboard, but she could see Nick's crooked smile out of the corner of her eye. Her heart was behaving strangely again, with that slow thud that seemed to send her blood round in erratic, churning surges.

Nick shifted closer, very slightly. 'Abigail, would you——'

'Abby!' They were interrupted by a rather peeved voice that made them both jump and look up as if startled out of some private world. A young man of thirty or so stood by the car. Good-looking in a somewhat nondescript fashion, he had fair hair and blond eyebrows which were at that moment drawn together in a disapproving frown.

'Hello, Peter.' For a moment Abby had wondered who he was and now she hurried on, feeling absurdly guilty, 'Um, Nick, this is Peter Middleton. Peter, you probably recognise Nick Carleton.'

Peter merely nodded and muttered something with bad grace, but the American was not so easily dismissed. 'Hi!' Obviously amused by the younger man's hostility, Nick vaulted out of the car to shake hands and force him to exchange pleasantries. Despite the fact that his shorts and bright shirt were undeniably scruffy next to Peter's sober suit, Nick managed to look infinitely tougher, Abby couldn't help thinking as she gathered her carrier-bags from the back of the car.

As soon as he could, Peter turned back to her. 'Where have you been?' he demanded. 'I said I might call round for tea this afternoon. I've been waiting nearly half an hour.'

Abby suppressed a sigh. As there was no other man in her life, Peter seemed determined to view her as his personal property, no matter how much she insisted otherwise. She had long ago realised that it was useless to argue with him. 'I've been shopping in Turlbury,' was all she said. 'Nick very kindly gave me a lift back.'

'I could have driven you into Turlbury if you'd wanted,' said Peter huffily.

With a slanting smile at Abby, Nick leant against the gleaming bonnet, arms crossed casually and long brown legs stretched out before him. Abby found herself looking at the way the muscles corded his thighs and hurriedly tore her eyes away.

'I'm afraid it's my fault,' he was saying, not sounding at all sorry. 'I persuaded Abby to give me a quick tour of the church on the way back.'

'Of the church!' Peter looked at Nick as if he had admitted some bizarre and vaguely grotesque habit. 'I wouldn't have thought the church would have interested someone like you.'

Nick's eyes narrowed. 'I wouldn't have thought *you* would be in any position to know what I might or might not be interested in,' he said with some con- tempt, and, in sudden shame, Abby realised that she had been just as quick as Peter to judge Nick on his superficial image.

'I'll make some tea,' she said hurriedly.

Peter was eyeing Nick with hostility. 'I haven't time now,' he said ungraciously. 'I've got to get back to the office.'

'You're a realtor, aren't you?' Nick asked abruptly.

'An estate agent,' Peter corrected, still sullen.

'Sure, estate agent.' Nick rolled his eyes. 'Got any houses for sale round here?'

Abby and Peter looked at him in surprise. 'Are you interested in buying?' Peter asked, the thought of a substantial percentage obviously warring with his jealous dislike of Abby's neighbour.

'Maybe.' Nick shrugged, non-committal. 'It's just a thought. Perhaps you could send me some details?'

'Of course.' Peter struggled to remain professional.

'Great. Well, I'd better get on.' The devil was back in Nick's eyes as he shot a smile of pure mischief down at Abby. 'Are you free for dinner this evening, Abigail?'

Peter bristled. 'Abby's having dinner with me this evening,' he said, his jaw thrust forward aggressively.

Abby's grey eyes darkened with vexation, with Peter for daring to answer on her behalf, and with Nick for such a needlessly provocative invitation. It was perfectly obvious that he had only asked her to irritate Peter. Unfortunately she had run out of excuses, and had indeed agreed to have dinner with Peter that evening.

'Thank you anyway,' she refused stiffly.

'Another time, perhaps.' Nick didn't look exactly crushed with disappointment, she observed waspishly.

If only Peter had not appeared just then! What had Nick been about to say? He could have suggested going out another time, but it obviously didn't matter that much to him! One minute he was gazing into her eyes, tangling her up in his charm, the next he seemed as if he couldn't care less. Abby watched with resentment as, his face creased with amusement, Nick tossed the car keys in the air and strolled off to his cottage, whistling noisily.

'Oh, Liz, thank goodness it's you!'

At the sight of her friend's cheerful face, Abby pulled the door wide open and slumped against the jamb in exaggerated relief.

Liz looked amused. 'Why, who were you expecting? Frankenstein?'

'Worse—Peter Middleton!'

'Oh, dear, he's not still in hot pursuit, is he? Why don't you make me a cup of coffee and tell me all about it—I'm gasping!'

Obediently Abby led the way through to the kitchen. When the coffee was ready, the two girls went to sit in the sun on the stone steps leading up to the back garden.

Abby had a quick glance through the gate, but there was no sign of Nick. She had hardly seen him since their visit to the church. Not that the peace and quiet wasn't a blessed relief after the constant music blaring out or that ghastly whistling, but the cottage *had* seemed peculiarly empty recently. He hadn't made any attempt to ask her out again, and although she wouldn't want to go—of course not!—he might at least have had the good manners to follow up his invitation. Obviously he had just been amusing himself for an afternoon and had better things to do now. Abby told herself she didn't care and sought refuge in reminding herself of her old dislike.

'So he's being a real pain, is he?' Liz asked sympathetically.

'Who?'

Liz lifted an eyebrow. 'Peter. Isn't that who we were talking about?'

'Oh, yes. . .yes.' Guiltily, Abby realised that her thoughts had been wandering to Nick Carleton yet again. 'He won't leave me alone, Liz. It's awful. He's always ringing me up, or dropping round, or "accidentally" bumping into me in the village. It used to be bad enough before, but he's suddenly got incredibly possessive. It's got to the point where I dread going out in case I meet him. And every time the phone rings, or someone knocks at the door, I jump. Yesterday he found an excuse to speak to me five times!'

'It must be terrible, being so desired,' commented Liz with a grin.

'You can joke, but it is!' Abby heaved a despairing sigh. 'It sounds cruel, but he's so *boring*. I don't know why he wants me, he only ever wants to talk about himself anyway.' She sighed again. 'And he's got wet lips,' she added, as if that clinched the matter.

'Yeuch!' Liz gave a sympathetic grimace. 'Why can't you just tell him you don't want to see him any more?'

'I've tried, honestly I have, but he doesn't take any notice. He just carries on coming round, almost as if he thinks he's doing me a favour. He knows I don't go out very much, so I never have any excuse for not being available. I'm always here, and I can hardly refuse to let him in.'

'I would,' said the stronger-minded Liz, unable to resist adding, 'I always said you should go out more.'

'I don't see why Peter Middleton should drive me from my own home.' Abby plucked at a weed crossly.

Sipping her coffee, Liz pondered the problem. 'Why don't you tell him you've got a new boyfriend?'

Nick? For one awful moment Abby wondered if she had spoken aloud. She pushed it away, horrified at the wistful air to her thought. She didn't want anything to do with him—even if Nick had not already made it clear that he wasn't really interested in her. Recovering herself, she said, 'Like who? This is Stynch Magna, remember? Everyone would know in five minutes if I was going out with someone else. He'd soon realise it wasn't true.'

'Couldn't you pretend? Just borrow someone until Peter got the message?'

'Whom do you suggest?' Abby asked, her voice heavy with sarcasm. 'There aren't all that many single men around here, and, even if there were, I wouldn't know how to go about acquiring one.'

'Nonsense,' said Liz briskly. 'Don't underestimate yourself, Abby. If you let your defences down a bit, they'd be falling over themselves to ask you out. That prickly exterior of yours puts them off, that's all.'

'It didn't put Peter off,' Abby pointed out gloomily.

'Peter's too thick-skinned to notice anything. No, we need someone for you to work your charms on.' Liz warmed to her theme. 'Someone a bit more mature, maybe?'

Affectionately watching her friend's forehead wrinkled in concentration, Abby shrugged off treacherous thoughts of Nick. 'What about the Reverend Mr Bolton?' she suggested with mock solemnity.

A vision of the vicar, stout and balding, fussily cleaning his glasses, rose before them, and after a moment's silence both girls collapsed into giggles.

'You're not taking this seriously, Abby,' Liz complained when she had got her breath back. 'I know, what about John Stables?'

'He's just got engaged, hasn't he?'

'So he has. He won't do.' She brightened. 'Neil Fleming?'

'He's got a beard,' objected Abby.

'Oh, well, if you're going to be *that* fussy. . .'

'I could always run off with Mike,' Abby suggested slyly, and laughed as Liz sat bolt upright.

'You leave Mike alone. I had enough trouble getting him to the altar as it was!'

As Liz had only succumbed after years of patient wooing on Mike's part, Abby merely grinned and Liz lapsed back into deep thought.

Abby watched an ant busily trying to drag a crumb much larger than itself across the step. Its energy made her feel listless, and in penance she cleared a path for it back to the nest.

'Got it!'

Startled by Liz's sudden exclamation, Abby spilt some coffee on her bright green T-shirt. 'Got what?' she asked, dabbing ineffectually at the stain with a tissue.

'Your new lover! It's so obvious I don't know why I

didn't think of him immediately. Well, don't you want to know who it is?'

Abby's heart sank. She knew what Liz was going to say. 'Surprise me,' she said in a hollow voice.

'Nick Carleton, of course.'

CHAPTER FIVE

'No,' ABBY said flatly, and then, when Liz looked surprised at her tone, 'Do you think people would really believe me if I started boasting about my wild affair with our resident superstar? I'm hardly his type!' Catching the edge of bitterness that crept into her voice, she added in an attempt at lightness, 'The vicar would be more likely!'

Liz was momentarily cast down. 'Perhaps you're right. You might need a bit more evidence to back up your claim. Maybe it would be better just to pretend that you've fallen madly in love with Nick, and can't bear to see another man at the moment?'

'Absolutely not!' Liz's suggestion caught Abby on the raw and she flinched away from the thought. It was ridiculous; everyone knew she couldn't stand the man. 'Nick Carleton has quite a big enough ego as it is, without me adding to it. Quite apart from anything else, he's just not my type,' Abby went on, glad of the excuse to reassure Liz and herself of her dislike for the American. 'I like subtle intelligent men, men who want a woman with a brain and not just a body. Nick is loud, brash, and quite incapable of taking anything seriously. It would be quite uncharacteristic of me to fall in love with him. Anyway,' she finished, rather lamely, 'Peter would only insist on helping me to get over my embarrassing infatuation—you know what he's like.'

'Maybe you're right.'

'There's no maybe about it—I *am* right!'

But Liz was reluctant to give up her idea. She glanced under her lashes at Abby, sitting cross-legged on the lawn in a green T-shirt and turquoise shorts, her face vivid above the bright colours. As usual, the beautiful hair was pulled away from her face in a casual pony-tail, and her feet were bare.

'I don't suppose,' she said slowly, 'that you could ask Nick if he could pretend to be in love with you for a little while? If you don't want to pretend to be infatuated with him? That would help your pride, and it would certainly convince everyone, even Peter.'

Abby stared at her, genuinely appalled at the idea. She would die rather than remind Nick of his careless invitation. 'You suppose right, Liz! You don't seriously imagine that I could waltz up to Nick Carleton and ask him to drop all the starlets he has in tow so that he can take *me* out?' She had deliberately not told Liz about their visit to the church, but Nick's evident amusement at her reactions still rankled. 'He'd laugh himself silly!'

To her utter horror, a disembodied chuckle floated over the garden wall. The next instant Nick's dark face, split by a broad grin, appeared. He leant his elbows on the wall and looked down at Abby. 'I wouldn't laugh,' he assured her, green eyes dancing. 'I've had a lot worse offers in my time, I can tell you.'

Abby had sunk her face in her hands, but now, scarlet, she stared up at him accusingly. 'You've been eavesdropping!'

'Got it in one, Abigail! But then, what do you expect from someone loud and brash?' Nick was obviously enjoying her discomfiture. 'Actually, I've been lying here trying to read this script, but your conversation was much more entertaining.' He directed a glinting smile at Liz. 'Mind if I join you?'

'I suppose that means you're coming round anyway,' Abby muttered, but none the less stomped off to put the kettle on again while Nick leapt over the wall and exerted all his charm in introducing himself to Liz. By the time she came out bearing fresh coffee, the two of them were obviously fast friends, and even Elijah was sucking up, Abby noted sourly, as the tabby rubbed himself against Nick's hand.

'We've been talking about your problem,' Nick announced, stretching himself out on the grass and taking the mug of coffee she offered with a smile of thanks.

'Oh?' Abby's tone was hardly encouraging.

'Nick thinks my idea is quite a good one,' Liz said smugly.

'Really? Which particular good idea, Liz?'

'You know, you and Nick pretend you're madly in love. If Peter sees you together, he won't have any choice but to believe that you don't want to go out with him.'

'I may be American, but at least I don't have wet lips or a beard,' Nick added. 'Surely that makes me eligible as one of your suitors?'

'Very funny.' Abby resumed her place on the steps and picked up her own mug. When the silence lengthened expectantly, she looked from one to another in surprise. 'This *is* a joke, isn't it? You're surely not taking this ridiculous idea seriously?' She had taken the opportunity to get herself under control in the kitchen and was pleased with her air of cool unconcern.

'Why not?' Liz demanded, affronted. 'If you really want to get rid of Peter, this is as good a way as any. Better, probably. And the beauty of it is, it's so reasonable,' she pointed out with a sideways look at Nick. 'Let's face it, even someone like Peter is going to understand why you would fall in love with Nick.'

Abby tensed despite herself and a wave of colour swept up her cheeks, but Nick merely chuckled. 'Thanks for the compliment, Liz. Unfortunately, it's Abby who wouldn't find it reasonable. You find me very resistible, don't you, Abigail Smith?'

There was an odd note in his voice, and Liz watched with interest as Abby said stiffly, 'It's not that. I know what Liz means. It just doesn't seem very likely that someone like you would be interested in *me*.' She wished they had never started this conversation!

There was a pause, then Nick sat up and said softly, 'It seems quite feasible to me.'

Looking from one to the other, Liz said quickly, 'Oh, come on, Abby. It solves the Peter problem, and, quite apart from that, it'll give the whole village something to talk about!'

'It's only for the summer,' Nick added persuasively.

Abby shifted, uneasily aware that things were getting out of hand. 'This is silly!' She attempted a laugh. 'You don't need to get involved with my problems, Nick.'

Green eyes flickered briefly. He shrugged, smiling. 'I'm an actor—think of it as good practice for me! Also, I'll be honest with you, it appeals to my sense of humour. I didn't care much for Peter, but if I were him I'd rather think you'd fallen for someone else than have to accept I was a dead bore. We wouldn't be doing any harm, as we both know where we stand, but we might have a lot of fun stirring everyone up!'

Is that all it would mean to him—*a lot of fun*? While Abby hesitated, obscurely hurt, Nick assumed a virtuous expression. 'And I know you don't approve of me spending the summer doing nothing, so I may as well make myself useful to you. What do you say?'

Abby thought of a summer dodging Peter Middleton. It would be so easy to take up Nick's offer. His corroboration would surely ensure that Peter got the message and it would be such a relief not to dread every knock at the door. Temptation beckoned dangerously and her pulse quickened at the thought of spending more time with Nick even as her mind shied away in alarm. Better by far to keep her distance. Nick Carleton had disturbed her peace of mind enough. The warning bells jangled insistently but still she hesitated, half appalled that she had even considered the idea.

'Well?' Nick prompted. 'Have we a deal?'

Later Abby would wonder what madness had seized her. She had decided to say no. It was a silly, embarrassing idea, of course it was. Why then did she suddenly hold out a hand with a smile that lit up her grey eyes and made Nick blink? 'Deal!' she said.

'Deal!' Nick repeated with a broad grin, taking her hand and drawing her irresistibly towards him. Before she could protest, he put his other hand under her chin, turned her face up to his, and dropped a careless kiss on her wide, inviting mouth.

At his touch Abby's lips parted in soft surprise, and

for a second, a lifetime, she forgot everything except Nick and the overwhelming feel of him. It was as if she had been waiting forever for this moment. His kiss was electrifying, a surge of sensation that washed over her, leaving her whole body quivering and her mind defenceless against its dangerous, insidious delight. She leant irresistibly into him, as her hand went up to touch his cheek by instinct. She could feel his fingers tighten on her as the dizzying pleasure spiralled between them, and then, suddenly, he released her.

Abby's eyes were huge and grey and Nick pulled his eyes away from their dazed look with an effort. He was breathing very carefully and his laugh was, for once, a little uncertain.

'That's called sealing a bargain.'

Abby couldn't look at him but she was aware of his every movement. She felt disjointed, unfocused, still giddy with remembered pleasure and sick at the abrupt return to reality. Liz was watching her with an expression of concern, and she pulled herself together, risking a glance at Nick. He was lying back on the grass, hands under his head, apparently relaxed and quite unperturbed. A man like that wouldn't think anything of a brief kiss, of course. . .Abby forced a bright smile. 'When do we start?'

Liz immediately became very matter-of-fact. 'You ought to go out to dinner. You need to be seen in public so that Peter hears the gossip before he sees Abby again.'

'Fine. We'll go out tonight.' Nick raised himself on one elbow. 'Liz, you're our agent. Where should I take Abby out to dinner?'

'Chez Florimonde,' Liz said promptly.

'Liz!' Abby was shocked. 'That's the most expensive restaurant in Oxfordshire!'

'Exactly. Where else would Nick Carleton take a girl? He'd hardly take you down to the Duke's Head for a pie and a pint, would he?'

'Well, I've enjoyed a few drinks down there already, but you're definitely right, Liz. Chez Florimonde it is.' Nick jumped to his feet. 'I'll go and make a reservation right now.'

'You'll never get a table,' Abby prophesied with some relief, feeling that things were going a little too fast. Surely all they need do was go to the pub together? There was no need for dangerously intimate dinners. 'You have to book about six months in advance to get in there.'

'They'll give *me* a table,' Nick said confidently. 'You go find yourself something smart to wear. You look gorgeous in those shorts, but I guess the restaurant wouldn't like it if you went like that. I'll see you later.' With a grin and a wave, he vaulted over the gate and disappeared into his cottage.

Feeling as if her world had been turned upside-down, Abby stared after him. She knew that Liz was longing to discuss that brief, endless, meaningless, marvellous kiss, but she couldn't talk about it yet. 'Why does he always have to jump over that gate?' she demanded before Liz could speak, glad that her confusion faded to comfortingly familiar exasperation as she watched him go. 'It's perfectly easy to open it!'

By the time she was finally ready, at seven-thirty, Abby had already changed her mind a dozen times about embarking on the pretence of a relationship with

Nick Carleton. She knew she should take the whole thing light-heartedly as he was doing, but every time she thought about that kiss her nerves fluttered, and the safe, sensible side of her nature protested in warning. But it was too late to get out of this evening now. Much to her regret, Nick's prediction that the restaurant would make a table available had been proved right.

Her budget did not allow her many smart dresses, so choosing something to wear was not a problem. Abby was glad she possessed at least one outfit which would not look out of place in such an expensive restaurant.

It had been an impulse buy one rainy day in Oxford, and she had afterwards scolded herself severely for such extravagance, for she had certainly not had much occasion to wear such a dress in Stynch Magna, but for now it was perfect. It was a simple dress, with a touch of frivolity suggested in the swirl of silken pleats which fell from the hips, but the deep amber colour flattered her skin and the delicate material was deliciously cool.

Normally Abby wore little make-up, but tonight she had accentuated the smokiness of her wide grey eyes with eyeshadow and mascara, and added a touch of colour to her generous mouth to bolster her confidence. Fastening her grandmother's topaz drop earrings in her ears, she studied her reflection critically. It was so long since she had dressed up that she hardly recognised the elegant creature in the mirror. The glossy chestnut hair curling to her shoulders gave her an abandoned look. In response to an inner prompting, she swept it up into a knot. There, that makes me

look older and more capable, she thought, oblivious
to the way it accentuated the long line of her neck.

Would Nick like the effect? she wondered, and then
caught herself up sternly. It didn't matter if he did or
not. This was just a game they were playing. . .wasn't
it? Abruptly Abby turned away from the mirror. The
whole thing was a stupid idea. Why on earth had she
agreed to it? She would go out with Nick this once,
just to keep Liz quiet, but at the restaurant she would
explain to Nick that she had changed her mind.

When the doorbell rang at last, Abby jumped and
her heart began to thump uncomfortably as she forced
herself to walk slowly downstairs. What was the matter
with her? It was only Nick Carleton. She took a deep,
steadying breath as she turned the handle. Only Nick
Carleton.

But it was not Nick. Peter stood on the step and
looked at her in astonishment.

'Abby! You look very smart. Are you going out?'

'Well, yes, I——'

'Out with Liz and Mike?' Peter asked, stepping
forward so that Abby was obliged to let him in.

'No, actually——'

'Abby?' For once Nick's timing was perfect. With a
tiny sigh of relief, Abby heard the deep American
voice from the kitchen, and the next moment he
appeared, bending his head slightly to get through the
old doorway. 'Abby, are you ready?' He broke off as
he noticed Peter.

Abby knew that she ought to say something to break
the frozen silence with which Peter had greeted Nick's
appearance, but she stood as if rooted to the spot.
Nick in scruffy shorts and T-shirt was impressive

enough, but here in dinner-jacket and bow-tie he looked magnificent. His dark good looks seemed to fill the tiny hallway, squeezing the breath from her body.

Abby finally found her voice with an effort. 'Er—I think you met Nick the other day, didn't you, Peter?'

Peter looked as if he had just been forced to swallow something unpleasant, but Nick merely nodded casually at him. 'Sure. You were going to send me details of some houses.' Without waiting for Peter to reply, he turned back to Abby. 'I hope you don't mind me coming in the back way?'

'Not at all.' Realising how ridiculously formal she sounded, she added, 'Of course not.'

'Why didn't you tell me you were free tonight?' Peter stared at Abby accusingly.

Nick looked at him with dislike. 'She's not free. She's having dinner with me.'

'But when I asked you this morning, you said you didn't feel like going out,' Peter persisted and Abby flushed.

'I'm afraid I changed my mind.'

'I wouldn't take no for an answer,' Nick added smoothly, letting his hand linger caressingly on her back. Abby was acutely aware of his touch burning through the thin silk. 'We're going to be late, honey,' he hinted.

Abby reminded herself that he was an actor. That warm, possessive look in his eyes was only part of the act. Now, if ever, was the time to deny the story he and Liz had concocted. She glanced at Peter. He wore an aggrieved look and his lower lip was thrust out petulantly. It wasn't really fair on him to persist with this charade with Nick. She could tell him now that it was only a joke. . .

Instead she said awkwardly, 'I'm ready. Sorry, Peter, but we must go. The table's booked and we mustn't be late.'

'Don't worry, I'm going,' Peter said in an injured tone. At the door, he turned back to Abby. 'Next time you change your mind, perhaps you'd let *me* know!'

Chez Florimonde overlooked the river and they had a cocktail on the terrace before the meal. Nick made her try a margarita, and Abby sipped the bitter drink cautiously as they leant against the railings and gazed out over the still water. Two swans floated by, sublimely indifferent to the busy dabbling of the ducks. On the far side of the river the willows trailed their branches disconsolately in the water.

Inside, Abby felt as if she had walked into a conservatory. There were plants everywhere, cunningly arranged to give tables privacy. Everything was pastel green or pink or white, glass and silverware gleamed in the candlelight and the room hummed with murmured conversations and the chink of knives on plates.

A subdued rustle of interest greeted Nick's entrance. Presumably people who could afford to eat here were used to seeing celebrities, Abby thought a trifle sourly. None the less, she was conscious of being watched enviously as Nick took her elbow and steered her to their table by the window in a secluded corner.

'Don't you mind people staring at you like that?' she asked Nick when the waiter had handed them the menus and vanished discreetly.

'Did you mind it?' he countered.

'They weren't looking at *me*.'

'Weren't they? All the men certainly were. I had to glare at several.' He smiled at Abby's expression of disbelief. 'It's true. I've never met a girl who's so unaware of her own beauty as you, Abigail.'

Abby opened her menu with fumbling fingers. 'Don't be silly,' she managed. 'I don't suppose anyone even noticed me next to the famous Nick Carleton!'

'I hate to disagree with you, Miss Smith, but you are quite wrong. But in answer to your question, no, I don't mind people recognising me. It's not very fashionable to enjoy being famous, but I like it. It means I have the money to do what I want and I can choose to do movies that interest me. It's not all that much fun being a struggling actor—you soon forget artistic integrity when it's a question of being able to pay the rent for another month.'

'But don't you resent the lack of privacy? I'd hate people to point and stare at me like that!'

'You're a very private person. I like meeting people. Being famous means you don't have to go through all the ritual when you meet someone for the first time— everyone immediately assumes they know you already! I guess it bugs me sometimes when people leap to conclusions about me.'

'Like I did?' Abby looked at him with direct grey eyes.

He hesitated. 'Perhaps. But then I made assumptions about you too.'

Their eyes met for a moment of charged silence, then Abby's eyes dropped to the menu. 'I'll have the salmon terrine to start with, please.'

It was a delicious meal, exquisitely presented on large white plates. Abby viewed everything with an artist's eye and approved of the way the colours of each dish were subtly combined for the maximum effect, the whole finished off by a carefully placed garnish. Nick was less enthusiastic.

'They must think I'm on a diet or something,' he complained, eyeing his tiny portion with disfavour. 'I could do with a big, juicy burger right now—with fries!'

'Just the all-American boy,' Abby mocked lightly, but she had noticed that he ran an expert eye over the wine list and selected an unpretentious label which none the less perfectly complemented the meal. She took a sip now and eyed him over the rim of her glass. 'Do you deliberately cultivate your image?'

He grinned. 'What image is that, Abigail?'

'You're so. . .American.'

Nick leant forward, suddenly serious. 'As far as I'm concerned, I don't have an image, Abby. I like hamburgers, I like fine wines. I don't see that those things are mutually exclusive. I happen to like wearing fun clothes. I'm afraid that's just me. The problem is that *you* have an image of me based on some prejudices you have against Americans—I don't know why. I am not ashamed of being American, but it's not something I cultivate deliberately as you're suggesting. The fact is that I grew up like any normal boy in Colorado. I always wanted to be an actor, but I sure didn't get discovered overnight like they always do in the books. I had to work hard to get where I am today.' He shrugged. 'The fact that *Carver* took off unexpectedly was a lucky break. If it hadn't I'd still be looking for an agent, but I'd be the same guy—I just wouldn't be able to afford the good wines!'

Reaching across the table, he took her hand and Abby felt a jolt that was becoming uncomfortably familiar. She tried to draw her hand away, but he held it tightly against the pale green linen tablecloth. 'Would you feel differently about me if I threw away all my shirts, Abigail?'

'I might if you could learn to call me Abby instead of Abigail!' Unreasonably flustered, she tugged her hand away.

The intent look vanished from his eyes, and he sat back with a grin. 'Couldn't you at least be like other girls and learn to love me for my money?'

'That's probably exactly what Peter will think.'

'He ought to know you better than that,' Nick said gently. At the warm smile in his eyes, Abby's heart began to thump slowly and painfully against her ribs and she was relieved when he looked away to catch a passing waiter's attention with the barest lift of an eyebrow. 'What about something else to eat—or would you prefer just coffee?'

'I'd like pudding *and* coffee, please,' she said with determined brightness. 'The chocolate cake sounds wonderful!'

Nick sounded amused. 'Most of the girls I take out just want to push a lettuce leaf around their plate.'

'I wish I had that kind of self-control,' Abby confessed as she dug her spoon into the deliciously moist cake, not wanting to know about all those other girls he had taken out. 'But I've got to go to the dentist tomorrow morning, so I'm eating extra now in case I can't tomorrow.'

'You don't need to make excuses. I like a girl with a

healthy appetite. There's something kind of erotic about seeing someone enjoy their food!'

Abby paused with the spoon halfway to her mouth. She glanced up, knowing that he was joking and trying to laugh back at him, but as their eyes met, and looked quickly away again, the laughter faded and trailed away into silence.

Abby put down her spoon uncertainly, unprepared for the rush of molten desire that dissolved her bones and left her burning with an aching need to reach across and touch him. She wanted to run her hands over him, she wanted to trace the laughter lines at the corner of his eyes, she wanted to wrap herself round him, breathe in the warm, masculine smell of him. There was a place where the pulse beat below his ear; she wanted to press her mouth to it. Horrified, Abby pushed her plate away with unsteady hands. Her appetite had gone.

The candle cast flickering shadows on Nick's face as he stirred his coffee with a brooding expression. Abby found her gaze dwelling on the firm contours of his face, at once peculiarly familiar and exciting. She felt as if the two of them were marooned together at this table, with only the warm candlelight and the soft silence between them.

A dribble of melted wax slid down the candle. Abby moulded it with her fingers, trying desperately to think of something to say, but her tongue felt dry and awkward. She swallowed, and, despite herself, her eyes slid back to Nick's mouth. Why choose this time to remember the feel of his lips? She picked up her wine glass and drained it, realising too late that it was already empty. Setting it down again with unwonted care, she ran her finger down the stem while her gaze skittered back to the hard line of his jaw.

Without warning, Nick lifted his head and looked straight into her eyes. Abby could not have turned away if she had tried. For long moments they stared at each other while the silence seemed to stretch and crackle with sudden tension. In the end it was Nick who spoke first, softly. 'Shall we go?'

Outside the night air was cool against Abby's face. They kept a good distance between them as they walked to the car in silence. Abby was preternaturally aware of everything: the whisper of silk against her legs, the click as Nick unlocked the car, the blue whiteness of his shirt against the dark jacket, the haunting scent of honeysuckle adrift in the darkness. . .

There was silence as the Rolls nosed its way out of the car park and into the dark country lanes, until Nick spoke suddenly out of the darkness.

'That guy who hurt you before—in the States—what was his name?'

'Stephen.' It was easier to talk about him than she had thought. 'I was very young, very unhappy. My mother had just remarried and I was still missing my father.' Abby's voice was distant as the memories crowded back. 'He worked for an international bank, and we always lived overseas, but he used to promise that we'd come back to England one day to live in the country. We used to come here for holidays. They were always such golden times.

'I couldn't believe it when my mother married Zack so soon after my father died and we went to live in Washington. Selfish of me, I suppose. My mother has a right to happiness as well, and she loves the parties and the social life there. I just wasn't prepared to try to like it.' It was the first time Abby had admitted as much to herself and she glanced at Nick. She knew he was listening, but he said nothing, so she went on.

'Stephen. . .' She paused. 'Well, Stephen was charming and good-looking, and I amused him for a while. I suppose I was different from the other girls he knew. I'd never been in love before, and I obviously didn't know how to play the game properly.'

'What game?' Nick asked.

Abby sighed. 'The dating game. The career game. The Washington game. Zack was—is—an influential man, and Stephen was. . .very ambitious. I was too naïve to realise that. Unfortunately for Stephen, my mother's marriage broke up quite soon. I think she probably married Zack on the rebound after Dad died. Anyway, she and Zack were divorced quite amicably. Poor Stephen!' Abby's smile was crooked. 'It turned out that he'd been wasting his time after all. An unknown English widow's daughter is not quite the same thing as Zack's stepdaughter. Stephen just vanished from my life overnight.'

'Didn't you ever see him again?'

'Once. Just before——' Abby broke off.

'Just before what?' Nick prompted.

'It doesn't matter.' She stared out through the windscreen, but she wasn't seeing the road. 'It doesn't matter,' she said again.

'OK.' Nick's voice was gentle. 'Thank you for telling me, Abby. I'm sorry it had to happen to you. Nobody needs a lesson like that.'

Abby turned to look at him, surprised at her own

sense of relief at having told him. 'Actually, I think it helped to talk about it. I didn't think it would, but it does.'

'Good.' That was all Nick said, but Abby knew that he wouldn't ask her any more. Obscurely grateful, she turned back to look out of her window as Nick leant over to slot a cassette into the machine. Music from *La Traviata* came spilling out of the speakers and Abby raised her eyebrows.

'Opera's not your usual style.'

'No.' He glanced at her and his smile gleamed briefly in the reflected lights on the dashboard. 'But then, neither are a lot of the things I like most.'

The car gathered speed as the languid, irresistible voice rose and fell, the music swelling to fill the car. Abby let it wash over her, and the blood began to beat insistently in her veins. When the last notes died away, she sat, excruciatingly aware of Nick so close beside her. He was only a matter of inches away. She could stretch out her hand and touch him now. Fiercely, Abby clasped her fingers together. This was madness!

He's American, this is just a game he's playing, you don't like him, not really, she repeated to herself, risking a sidelong glance at Nick. He was staring straight at the road ahead with a slight frown, almost forbidding in his immaculate dinner-jacket.

Abby felt a desperate need to shore up her crumbling resistance. Was she just like all those other girls, a pushover for the price of a meal and the warm light in a pair of green eyes? She longed to be home and away from the dangerous attraction of the man beside her.

As the car drew up outside, the light in her doorway

seemed to beckon as a safe harbour. Nick switched off the engine and in the echoing quiet turned in his seat to watch her profile.

Despite herself, Abby tensed.

'Relax,' he said softly. 'I grew out of making passes in the front seat years ago.'

It was easier to deal with the familiar, mocking Nick. Abby lifted her chin proudly. 'I'm glad to hear it.'

'Quite apart from anything else, English cars just aren't designed for it. It must have been some moralist who thought of putting the shift in between the seats like that!' He opened his door, but forestalled Abby as she reached for her own door-handle. 'Wait, let me.'

Moments later he opened her door for her with a flourish. 'You see, we Americans do have some manners!'

Unable to think of a suitable reply, Abby gave a stiff smile. 'Thank you.'

Nick was very close, blocking her way to the gate, and unconsciously she stepped back against the car. Pushing the door shut with a click, he moved to place one hand firmly on either side of her.

Pinned as she was against the bodywork, Abby's heart was pounding so loudly she was sure that Nick must hear it, but she said bravely, 'I thought you'd grown out of kissing girls in cars.'

'I have.' Green eyes glinted in the moonlight. 'But only in the front seat. I didn't say anything about kissing them *against* cars!'

She had plenty of time to move. She could have pushed him away if she had tried. But instead Abby stood, ensnared by desire, while Nick's hands slid slowly up her arms and lingered on her shoulders as he looked down into her eyes.

'Your skin is like silk,' he said, his voice deep and warm, and then his hands were cupping her face and he was bending his head with agonising slowness to capture her mouth with his own.

At the first touch of his lips, so warm, so sure, all of Abby's carefully constructed defences collapsed, scattered like straws in the wind. Her fingers spread against his chest, feeling the beat of his heart beneath his shirt, as she gave back kiss for kiss in the glorious relief of giving in.

The fire that had been smouldering all evening was burning high now. Their kisses deepened and Nick's hands left her face to run caressingly up and down her spine, the smooth material of her dress slithering against her skin as he gathered her closer. Abby was breathless with his kisses, but her arms were about his neck, her fingers tangling in his crisp dark hair. Her hands had a life of their own, touching him, feeling him, as she was sucked into a vortex of desire and at last, at last, she could kiss that pulse below his ear and the irresistible line where jaw met throat.

'Abby, Abby,' Nick murmured against her neck, and she shivered at the naked desire in his voice. 'You're so cool, so warm.'

Her eyes were dark with longing as he pulled out her combs, loosening the thick, glossy hair with his fingers and letting it tumble about her shoulders in luxuriant abandon.

'I've been wanting to do that all evening.' Burying his hands in her hair, he bent to kiss her again, letting his lips drift over her face and throat until Abby felt she would dissolve with wanting him.

'Nick. . .' It was hardly more than a breath, but he drew back slightly to brush a few strands of hair away from her face with a tenderness that made Abby ache.

'What is it, Abigail Smith?' His voice was very low and his smile very warm as he searched her face with his eyes.

'I——' Abby turned her head restlessly. Impossible to explain how she felt. Impossible to ask him to stop, when she never wanted him to let her go.

At that moment a car came round the bend into the lane, the noise of its engine abrasive in the sweet stillness of the night, its headlights pinioning them in a blinding glare for a few seconds before it swept past.

The moment too was past.

'I guess I nearly forgot what an old-fashioned girl you are,' Nick said, releasing her reluctantly. Abby leant weakly against the car, still giddy with whirling sensation.

'I nearly forgot too.' She tried to smile. 'I'd better go in.' Her legs were still shaky as she forced herself upright. 'Thank you for a lovely evening, Nick.'

'Abby——' Nick put out a hand as if to stop her, but she was gone.

CHAPTER SIX

ABBY woke wondering why she felt edgy and unsettled. She lay and watched the dust dancing in a shaft of sunlight through the curtains, blinking away sleep until her mind cleared and focused with a jolt of memory.

She sat up abruptly, then sank back against the pillows, staring blindly at the dress she had worn last night, limp and discarded over the back of a chair. The memory of it sliding beneath Nick's hands was so vivid that she squirmed. Surely—*surely*—she hadn't responded with such abandon? Not cool, collected Abigail Smith? Unconsciously she touched her fingers to her mouth and then gazed at them, as if amazed that Nick's kiss was not imprinted there.

What had she done? Restlessly she threw back the sheet and went to draw back the curtains. Her stomach lurched as she saw the Rolls, still parked where Nick had kissed her, and the thought of his hard body pressing her against the car shivered down her spine, setting a thousand butterflies aflutter and staining her cheeks with a flush which was half horrified embarrassment, half exhilaration.

She had no idea what she would do when she saw Nick and for perhaps the only time in her life was glad of the excuse of her dentist's appointment. She still retained a fear of dentists which she confessed was childish and unreasonable, but the thought of facing

Nick that morning and pretending that nothing had happened was even worse. Quietly, she slipped out of the cottage.

As the bus lurched and swayed along the country lanes into Turlbury, Abby's mind flitted nervously between the dentist and the previous night. It was almost a relief to reach the dental surgery and be shown into the waiting-room, empty except for a couple, obviously mother and daughter, who were leafing through magazines in a desultory fashion. Abby gave them a mechanical smile as she went to perch nervously on a cracked and sagging leather armchair.

It was ridiculous to feel nervous about going to the dentist at her age, she told herself sternly, as the unmistakable whine of a drill rose and fell behind a closed door. With studied casualness, she got to her feet and tried to fix her attention on a series of old hunting prints, all equally devoid of interest, but in the end was forced to the table in the corner, which was piled high with tattered and ancient magazines.

'There must be something here less than five years old,' she muttered irritably to herself. The whine of the drill paused, then resumed with renewed fanaticism. Half-heartedly selecting a copy of *Punch*, a mere eighteen months old, she resumed her seat and began to turn the pages mindlessly.

'Sounds as if Jason's having a few fillings,' the mother commented to her daughter. 'I told him not to drink all that nasty lemonade.'

But the girl had at last found something of interest in the magazine and was unconcerned about her brother. 'Look, Mum.' She folded back a page and showed the article to her mother. 'Remember I was telling you about him the other day?'

'Is that the one who's supposed to be staying round here?'

'Nick Carleton. Sharon said she saw him in Turlbury, and he smiled at her, but I bet she's lying.' The girl sniffed suspiciously. 'Even if he is staying around here, he wouldn't take any notice of Sharon! It's got pictures here of all his girlfriends. None of them look much like Sharon, do they?'

Her mother laid down her own magazine and leant over to get a better view. 'He can't have been out with *all* of them, surely?'

'It says here, "His name has been linked with some of the world's most beautiful women."' She tapped one of the photos. 'She's lovely, isn't she? I wouldn't mind looking like her.' Her eye skimmed down the page. 'Oooh, I didn't know *she* was one of his girlfriends—I thought she was married to that singer.'

'I don't think marriage makes much difference to people like that,' the woman said. 'Who's that one with him, then?'

Abby was trying desperately to concentrate on an article about office Christmas parties, but the words danced before her eyes.

'That's Charlotte Canning.' The girl sighed at her mother's ignorance. 'She's his latest. Oh, look, it says here——'

To Abby's intense frustration, she broke off as the door opened and a mutinous-looking boy of twelve or so came in. Presumably this was the unfortunate Jason, for the girl and her mother stood up and began gathering their bags together.

For the fifteenth time, Abby reread the first sentence about the dreaded Christmas parties. The girl's discarded magazine lay where she had tossed it on to a chair. It seemed to draw Abby's eyes and hastily she looked away to stare with spurious interest at a dusty spider plant on the mantelpiece.

At last they were gone. As soon as the door had closed, Abby cast aside the *Punch* and snatched up the other magazine.

Nick's face smiled glossily up at her from the cover. Why hadn't she remembered that self-satisfied expression before she had let him kiss her like that last night? Thumbing her way through the magazine, she searched for the offending article. So Nick had been linked with the world's most beautiful women, had he? What did he think he was doing with Abigail Smith?

This must be it! Abby's eyes narrowed at the array of photos of Nick with a seemingly endless parade of beauties on his arm, all of them clinging to him with wide, dazzling smiles. What on earth did he see in such simpering toothpaste advertisements? Abby wondered malevolently, but even she had to admit that Charlotte Canning was something out of the ordinary, with that swinging curtain of blonde hair and dazzlingly blue eyes. The main picture was of Nick and Charlotte in a scene from the film Abby had seen. Charlotte was looking meltingly up at Nick as he bent to kiss her.

The scene was bitterly reminiscent of last night. Had it really been just another pose for Nick?

Angrily Abby dashed away the sudden sting of tears and concentrated on the article.

Nick Carleton's name has been linked with some of the world's most beautiful women, but more recently it has been the lovely Charlotte Canning who has been seen most often at his side. I met them both on the set of *Tomorrow You Die*, and the relationship between them is obviously close.

Why has Nick never married? 'I've been waiting for the right woman,' he smiles, but there is a serious look in his eyes. 'I've been out with lots of gorgeous girls, and enjoyed every minute, but I know that when the right woman comes along, that will be it.' And is Charlotte Canning the right woman? They insist that they are just good friends, but exchange a warm and secret smile that excludes the rest of the world. Charlotte Canning is a very lucky lady!

Well, what had she expected? Abby's face twisted as she reached the end of the article, and in a moment of blind fury at herself, she hurled the magazine across the room. 'You fool!'

'Miss Smith?' The receptionist, appearing silently in the doorway, looked at her with some concern.

Retrieving the magazine guiltily and dropping it back on to the table, Abby followed her out of the room. For once she hardly noticed the dentist's poking and probing and even made no protest when he announced that a filling needed replacing. She was far too preoccupied with self-recrimination.

How could she have come so close to making a fool of herself over Nick? It wasn't as if she hadn't had the experience of Stephen to warn her against that kind of practised charm. Those kind of men were all the same. Why had she told him about Stephen? Like Stephen, Nick had just been amusing himself—he had even *told* her that he found the idea of pretending to be in love with her amusing. Abby writhed as she remembered how passionately she had responded to his kiss. How he must have laughed to have seen how easily she had succumbed!

Well, it would be a short-lived victory. She had no intention of allowing it to happen again.

Emerging from the dentist with one side of her jaw still frozen, she ran slap into Peter Middleton.

'Don't you have your escort with you this morning?' he greeted her peevishly.

Abby had almost forgotten that Peter was the original reason for her date with Nick. She shook her head. 'Not this morning.'

Peter immediately began to look hopeful, and her heart sank. 'I suppose you wouldn't want to see too much of him,' he said. 'These Americans are so wearing, aren't they?' He kept step with her as she turned to walk down the street. 'Still, it was nice of you to take pity on him and keep him company for an evening.'

Of course, Peter would think up an explanation like that! Abby almost laughed out loud at the thought of Nick needing anyone's pity. 'It wasn't quite like that,' she said, realising as soon as she opened her mouth that she had once again missed a perfect opportunity to deny Liz's absurd story and put an end to the need for her to pretend any sort of relationship with Nick.

Peter laughed indulgently. 'Ah, I know you too well, Abby! I quite share your views on Americans, which makes your neighbourliness doubly admirable.' Abby gritted her teeth as he went on, 'I have to confess I was a teensy bit jealous last night, but of course I soon realised what must have happened.'

'Oh?' She stared at him, hardly able to believe his complacency.

'I assume he must have taken advantage of your kind heart, and put you in a position where you found it impossible to refuse. It must have been a dreadful bore listening to him talk about himself all evening.'

That was rich, coming from Peter! Nick was many things, but he certainly wasn't a bore. Abby lengthened her stride. 'I had a very enjoyable evening,' she said coldly.

'That's like you to say that.' Peter hurried to keep up with her. 'In any case, you've done your duty now. Perhaps you could spare an evening for me now,' he said with an attempt at jocularity.

It seemed as if she was back at square one. Obviously it would take more than one evening out with Nick to convince Peter that he was not wanted. Abby now found herself in a dilemma. She could call an end to the pretence with Nick and to any chance of a repeat of last night's humiliation, but that would leave her open once more to Peter's constant pestering. Or, she acknowledged reluctantly, she could carry on with the pretence and make it very plain to Nick that a pretence was all it was.

Abruptly she made up her mind. 'I can't tonight, Peter. I'm going out with Nick.'

'Again?'

'Yes,' she said firmly, casting any lingering doubts to the wind, and changing the subject before he had time to protest further. 'Are you going to send him any details about houses for sale?'

'I put something through his door this morning,' he said with a touch of sulkiness. 'There isn't much on the market at the moment. Look, let me at least drive you home if I can't see you tonight.'

'There's no need. I can quite easily get the bus.'

'But the Escort is just round the corner. . .'

'It's really not necessary,' Abby repeated and glanced at her watch. 'I must rush.'

She left him staring after her as she hurried away. It was impossible not to compare Peter with Nick, who had simply ignored her refusal and swept her off bodily into his car. Peter was so stolid, so boring, so lacking in the electrifying atmosphere that Nick seemed to carry around with him. Nick was infuriating, unsettling. He was insincere, superficial, and smug—but, when he was near, everything was somehow in sharper focus and she felt alive and aware in a way that she had never known before. Abby paused in the street, trying to remember what it had been like before Nick had swept into her life. She had been comfortable then, content with her security, but would contentment be enough now? Abby thought of Charlotte Canning's perfect features and pushed aside the memory of Nick's kiss.

Contentment would just have to be enough.

When she got home, Nick was sitting in her kitchen, his feet propped on the table, reading the details Peter had left for him. Abby had sat on the bus convincing herself that it would be easy to ignore Nick, or at the very least keep him at arm's length, but at the sight of him her confidence faltered. Impossible to ignore the way her heart leapt and every pretence at indifference crumbled.

'Why don't you make yourself at home?' She took

refuge in sarcasm, dropping her handbag on to the table by his feet.

Nick grinned and swung his long legs unhurriedly to the floor. 'Where have you been? You look very cross!'

'I've been to the dentist.' She fixed him with a cold look. 'What are you doing in here?'

'I came in to find you.'

'I don't remember giving you a key!'

'Ah, but I've watched where you hide the spare,' he confessed shamelessly. 'And I ran out of coffee again!'

Abby was glad of the excuse to squabble. It was easier to pretend she didn't care. She began to put her shopping away with much banging of cupboard doors. 'You've got a nerve sometimes!'

'I didn't think you'd mind.' Nick watched her with some amusement.

'Well, I do!'

'Come on, Abigail, don't be cross.' He came up behind her and put his arms about her as she stood by the fridge, pressing a kiss to the side of her neck. His closeness enveloped her in hazy excitement and every sense quivered at the touch of his lips.

The urge to lean back against him was overwhelming. 'Don't,' Abby croaked.

'What's the matter?' Nick turned her round to face him, but she refused to meet his eyes. 'I thought we were supposed to be in love,' he teased.

'Only when someone's watching.'

There was a pause. 'No one was watching last night.'

A tide of colour surged up Abby's face and she wrenched herself out of his arms, turning back to stack the milk and orange juice clumsily in the fridge. 'I'd rather forget about last night.'

Nick leant against the fridge door with one hand, forcibly closing it, so that Abby was left clutching a carton of yoghurt and staring up into his face apprehensively. There was an unexpectedly grim look about his mouth.

'Now why would you want to forget about it, Abigail? I thought you enjoyed it.'

'I—I enjoyed the meal.'

'But not the kiss? Don't give me that! You enjoyed it as much as I did.'

Abby ran the tip of her tongue round lips that were suddenly dry. 'That wasn't in the agreement,' she said.

'What agreement?'

'That we would—er—pretend to be in love just to convince Peter that I wasn't interested in him.'

To her relief Nick moved away to prop himself against the kitchen table and watch her with folded arms. 'You may be old-fashioned, Abigail, but surely even you will admit that people don't fall in love, pretend or otherwise, without at least an occasional kiss?'

'I think Peter would get the message if he just saw us together,' she persisted stubbornly. 'I'll admit that I'm using you, but you volunteered. I'm just saying that I don't want you to forget that it *is* just a pretence.'

'So you want me to have the pleasure of taking you out, but not of touching you?'

There was a slight edge to his voice and Abby cringed inwardly. Then she remembered the string of girls in the magazine article, not to mention Charlotte Canning, whom he was presumably two-timing right at this moment. It wouldn't do Nick Carleton any harm to realise that he wasn't as irresistible as he thought he was!

She lifted her chin. 'Yes.'

'Are you sure you wouldn't rather just call the whole thing off?' This time the note of bitterness was unmistakable.

'Well, the thing is. . .' Abby hesitated, puzzled by his attitude. She wouldn't have thought he'd have cared one way or the other. 'The thing is that I met Peter this morning and. . .and I told him that you were taking me out tonight as well,' she finished in a rush.

Nick looked down at her for a moment. Abby found that she was holding her breath. 'All right, Abby,' he said at length, his smile rueful. 'Have it your own way. We'll do the thing on your terms—no hands!'

She hadn't expected him to be like this. She shifted uneasily. 'Of course, I quite understand if *you* would rather call it a day.'

'You mean, now that I've realised I'm not going to get my wicked way with you, I might not consider it worth my while?'

She flushed angrily at his tone. 'I'm sure there'll be no shortage of other applicants!'

'I might not be interested in other applicants.'

'You're not usually so fussy!' she snapped.

'Now what in the world do you mean by that?' He smiled, but it did not quite reach his eyes.

'Merely that the queue of those tried and tested stretches a long way back, doesn't it?'

'Ab-ee-gail! You haven't been listening to gossip about me, have you?'

'I understood it was common knowledge, rather than gossip,' Abby said.

Nick's green eyes narrowed. 'As the one most closely involved, I'd have thought that I would have been the one to know!'

They glared at each other for a moment, then he turned away to stare out of the window, the set of his shoulders still tense and angry, then he ran his hands through his hair with a short laugh. 'What is it about you, Abigail, that gets under my skin?' Turning back to her he grinned, once more the lazily good-humoured Nick she knew. 'Come on, stop scowling at me like that, and tell me what you think of these houses.' He pulled out a chair for her, and, after a moment's hesitation, she sat down and took the papers he handed to her.

'Are these the details Peter left for you?'

'That's right. The only one I like is this one.' He leant over and pointed it out, his arm brushing against hers. Abby concentrated fiercely on the photograph.

'That's Stynch Manor!'

'Is that the one in the painting you're working on? I thought it looked sort of familiar.'

'I think so. It would be interesting to compare the pictures.'

'Hey, it looks quite different now,' said Nick in the studio, looking from the photograph to the painting. The newly cleaned colours glowed on the canvas, and the features which had been hidden under the accumulated layers of dirt and grease now stood out clearly. They showed an old house, bathed in golden evening light, set serenely above a smooth sweep of lawn. In the foreground of the painting a couple sat beneath a tree, their heads close together and their fingers entwined, obviously in love. Abby looked at it and thought about Nick standing close beside her.

The estate agent's photograph in black and white looked dreary and prosaic in comparison, but it was undoubtedly the same house. The large windows looking out over the grounds were the same, as were the wings of the house, which were set at a wider angle than usual.

'It looks rather unloved now,' Abby commented, stepping away from Nick casually to put some distance between them. 'A house like that needs people living in it. Recently there's only been old Mr Mortimer and he was in a home for years before he died.'

'Shall we go and have a look round?'

'We?' Abby looked at him in surprise.

'Of course. Hell, it's a perfect opportunity to let Peter know how in love we are!' Nick looked down at her with a slight twist to his smile. 'I expect I can manage to convince him without actually throwing you across a bed!' When Abby only bit her lip, he went on, 'And anyway, I'd like your opinion.'

'I can tell you now that it's in a shocking state of disrepair,' she retorted. 'I don't suppose any work has been done on it for the last fifty years.'

'Let's at least go and see it,' he said persuasively, and in the end she gave in, curious to see the inside of the house after so many years.

That night she and Nick walked down to the Duke's Head for a drink. Nick had suggested going to the theatre in Oxford, but Abby was reluctant to spend another whole evening with him. He had not referred again to their argument, if it could be called that, but she was aware of a new coolness about him. He had left her alone all afternoon. Despite a day spent reminding herself that this was just what she wanted, Abby had been unable to shake off an aching feeling of unhappiness and obscure resentment that had made her sharp when Nick had finally appeared.

'Just a drink will be enough,' she said. 'It's only in case Peter calls round, after all.'

Nick looked at her for a moment, then shrugged. 'Sure, whatever you want.'

They were scrupulously polite to each other as they walked through the village to the pub. Nick kept his hands thrust into the pockets of his jeans, while Abby clutched the arms of the jumper she had slung round her shoulders against the slight chill of the evening. They were careful not to touch at all, although at the door Nick reached for her hand. 'We may as well give Peter something to think about if he's in here.'

Peter, unfortunately, was not in the pub, but there were plenty of raised eyebrows and significant looks at their entrance. The villagers were far too polite to stare, although Abby was perfectly well aware that the news that she and Nick had been seen holding hands would be all over the village by the morning.

Nick seemed to be on friendly terms with the barmaid, and exchanged greetings with many of the men leaning at the bar. There was much good-natured laughter as they tried to persuade him to try a pint of real beer, while Abby sat at a table and tried to forget the way he had dropped her hand as if it were a parcel. Eventually Nick managed to fight his way back to her, carrying a pint of lager and a gin and tonic.

'I tried that beer of theirs once,' he said, plumping down beside her. 'Never again!'

'Oh, look, there's Liz and Mike!' Abby waved frantically at her friend across the pub and pointed at the empty chairs by their table.

As Liz obediently wended her way through the press of people, with Mike in tow, Nick murmured in an undertone to Abby, 'For someone deeply in love, you seem very anxious for other people to join us.'

'If we were that in love, we'd have better things to do than sit in a pub!' she responded, her voice more bitter than she had intended.

He gave her a mocking look. 'How right you are! Hi, Liz.' He got to his feet and shook hands with Mike, a big, burly man with a genial face. 'Come and join us.'

'Do you think we should?' Liz asked doubtfully, echoing Nick's comment. 'You ought to prefer to be alone really.'

'Don't be silly, Liz.' Abby was anxious not to be alone with Nick. 'You can always tell people how we were only interested in each other, or something.'

'Help the gossip along a bit? Perhaps you're right.' Liz sent her long-suffering husband off to the bar for a drink and leant forward. 'How's it going? Has Peter twigged yet?'

Abby explained about her meeting with Peter that morning. 'This is act two now—except he's not here— and tomorrow Nick's asked him to show us round Stynch Manor.'

'That sounds excellent,' Liz approved. 'It's a lovely old house. The only time we're ever allowed in there is for the church fête every year. It's such a pity it's been allowed to go to rack and ruin. Oh, thank you, darling.' She took a sip of the vodka and orange Mike handed to her and turned back to Nick. 'Talking of the fête, I ought to warn you that the vicar is trying to pluck up the courage to ask you to open it this year, so you'd better be ready with your excuses.'

'What would I have to do, cut a ribbon or something?'

'You just stand up and make a little speech—oh, and give out the prizes at the end, of course.'

'Sounds fun. I wouldn't mind doing that.'

'Would you really? What a coup for Stynch Magna! Having Nick Carleton to open the fête should really pull in the crowds.' Liz sat back in her seat with a satisfied smile.

Mike shook his head at his wife. 'I ought to warn you that Liz is notorious for getting people to agree to do things they later learn to regret bitterly!'

'Hear, hear!' Abby said with feeling.

'It's all in a good cause,' Liz defended herself. 'The fact is that people will pay good money to see someone like Nick.'

'Don't make his head any bigger than it is already,' said Abby, folding her arms crossly.

Nick bared his teeth at her. 'My greatest fan!'

'Now, now, you two!' Liz shook her finger at them. 'You're not giving a very good impression of a couple in love. I thought you were supposed to be an actor, Nick! It's just as well Peter isn't here. He'd probably find it very encouraging!'

'Sorry, Liz!' Nick grinned, but Abby felt as if she was not included in his smile. 'What else do you want me to do at the fête?'

'Why don't you just raffle him off, Liz?' Abby suggested sourly. 'That ought to bring in a bit of cash!'

Liz paused with her drink halfway to her mouth, and looked at Abby with an arrested expression. 'Abby, what a brilliant idea!'

Abby groaned. 'Oh, no, what have I said?'

'I hate to break this to you, Liz,' Mike said kindly, 'but Nick isn't yours to raffle.'

'That's right, I'm afraid I belong to my agent!' Nick assumed a mournful expression.

'Be quiet, all of you!' Liz waved her drink at them. 'What if—and of course this is entirely up to you, Nick—what if we made you first prize in the raffle? Not all of you,' she added hurriedly.

'Thank you!' Nick mopped his brow.

'Just a bit of you. How much do you think girls would pay for a kiss from Nick Carleton?'

Abby and Mike stared at her, aghast. Nick looked at Abby. 'That rather depends on the girl, doesn't it? Abby here wouldn't pay a dime!'

Abby's stomach twisted at the undercurrent of bitterness in his voice and the unhappiness that had nagged all day hardened into a hard, insistent knot of pain.

Liz's quick glance flicked from Abby to Nick. 'Abby,' she said firmly, 'is a very unusual girl! You don't want to take any notice of her, Nick. I'll bet that if we offered a kiss from Nick Carleton as first prize in the raffle, every single female in the village would buy a ticket! It wouldn't have to be a proper kiss, just a peck on the cheek or something,' she added soothingly.

'You're not really going to agree to do this, are

you?' Abby demanded of Nick in an undertone, as he laughed.

'Why should you care? I took your point about preserving your pristine purity, but I didn't realise it extended to every other female in England. What is this, Year of the Virgin, or something?' His eyes were very cold.

Abby lifted her chin. 'It's just such a conceited idea, to think that someone would pay to kiss you.'

'It wasn't my idea, it was Liz's, if you remember. And if it helps raise some money to save that church, I don't see that it really matters.'

Liz and Mike exchanged speaking glances. 'It's only a bit of fun, after all.' Liz reached out and took Mike's hand. 'You won't mind if I buy a ticket, will you, darling?'

That dragged an unwilling laugh out of Abby, but the rest of the evening seemed interminable. Nick laughed and joked with Liz and Mike while Abby smiled mechanically and looked at everyone except Nick, aware of no one except Nick. He was ignoring her. Liz was right—all the girls would be queuing up at the chance of winning a kiss from him, but he obviously didn't care whom he kissed. Thin claws of unreasoning jealousy tightened round Abby's heart. Unconsciously she sighed.

Nick was watching her more closely than she realised. 'Come on, let's go. You look tired. If anyone asks, Liz, you can say we couldn't wait to be alone!'

He stood up and held out his hand, and Abby, for once, forbore to protest and let herself be pulled to her feet. The feel of his hand against the small of her back as he steered her towards the door was curiously comforting, but as soon as the door closed behind them, he dropped his arm and, as before, they walked home without touching. Nick seemed to be wrapped in his own thoughts, and the silence between them was cold.

Abby reminded herself of all the girls he must have escorted home in the dark, those girls with their toothy smiles and low cleavages. He wouldn't have had his hands in his pockets with *them*, that was for sure! She told herself she was glad that Nick was so willing to accept the distance she had set between them, and refused to wonder why she felt like crying when he merely wished her a cool goodnight and left her standing alone at the gate.

CHAPTER SEVEN

NICK had arranged to meet Peter outside Stynch Manor at eleven o'clock the next morning.

Peter's face, when he saw that Nick was accompanied by Abby, was a study in chagrin. 'I didn't know that you were coming as well,' he whispered to her while Nick strolled off to admire the outside of the house. Age had weathered the stone a golden grey, and moss grew unchecked on the paving stones beneath their feet. The great windows looked emptily out over the rolling grounds, now sadly neglected, though the great chestnut still stood as it had in the painting. Abby almost expected to see the two lovers entwined beneath its spreading branches.

'Come and look at this, honey,' Nick called to Abby over his shoulder, and rather reluctantly she went to join him, conscious of Peter watching her.

Nick slung a casual arm round her shoulders and pulled her towards him. Abby quivered in response to his touch, and in defence she stiffened. He looked down at her irritably.

'For heaven's sake, Abigail, loosen up! Peter will never get the message with you looking as if I've forced you here at gunpoint. Come on, put your arm round me.'

How could she relax when her whole body tingled at his nearness? When her blood pounded and every fibre of her being yearned to ignore her pride and lean against his solid warmth. After a moment's hesitation, she slipped her arm round his waist. 'Very good,' he said sarcastically. 'It's not so difficult really, is it?'

'I wish we'd never started this,' she muttered.

Nick looked pensively at a gutter hanging off the wall. 'I'm beginning to wish that too,' he said quietly.

Abby winced at the abrupt stab of misery, and made as if to draw away, but he pulled her back. His arm was iron-hard and unyielding against her. 'Don't go now, I think Peter might at last begin to realise that you're not interested in me just as a neighbour if we play it right today. Once he's got the message, we can call the whole thing off.'

She hadn't realised how strong he was. His arm was like an iron bar around her. To struggle would have been useless and undignified, so she stood next to him, looking wretchedly up at the façade of the house. Abby was achingly aware of Nick breathing where her hand rested on his denim shirt and her heart thudded painfully.

Abruptly Nick dropped his arm. 'Peter must have got the point by now.' Abby tried not to flinch at his coolness. This was what she had wanted, wasn't it? He was obviously bored by the whole affair, and by her. She stole a glance at his profile with a flicker of resentment. He was the one who had been so keen on the whole stupid idea, after all!

Peter's demeanour made it very obvious that he had indeed noticed their apparently casual embrace. Normally, Abby would have found his air of hurt formality an excruciating embarrassment, but she was too preoccupied by the new strain between her and Nick to spare Peter much notice, and even that lessened as she found herself gradually caught up in the enchantment of the house.

She and Nick wandered from echoing room to echoing room. Each was mustier and more dilapidated than the last, but nothing could disguise the graceful proportions, or the light that streamed in through the elegant windows. The house was crying out for someone to love it. Abby poked around the kitchen, mentally equipping it with her favourite pans. At one end was a huge inglenook, cold and bare, but it was so easy to visualise a flickering fire and a comfortable chair drawn up in front of it. Abby ran a hand along the great wooden beam and for a betraying moment allowed herself to imagine Nick sitting in the chair while she sat on the rug at his feet and leant her head against his knee.

Dreamily, hardly aware of the treacherous nature of her thoughts, she drifted over to join the two men who were inspecting the boiler. 'This is a beautiful house! It should have bowls of flowers and beeswax and masses of glossy white paint,' she enthused to Nick, the tension between them momentarily forgotten as they climbed the wide staircase. Her bright red dress was a vivid splash of colour against the damp-stained walls and dusty floors.

Peter cleared his throat. 'As you see, the house is in need of extensive renovation. It would need complete rewiring and replumbing, damp-proofing and, I imagine, a new roof. All these would necessitate considerable extra expense.'

'Not much of a salesman, are you?' Nick commented, looking round the ancient bathroom and grimacing at the sagging ceiling. 'Shouldn't you be talking about all the charm and character?'

'Those are, of course, features of the house,' Peter agreed stiffly.

Nick gave him a glimmering smile. 'Do you know of a reputable firm of architects?'

Peter's jaw dropped. 'You're not considering buying!'

'Maybe.' Nick was watching Abby. She had pushed open a window and was leaning out to look at the view, the sunlight warm on her face.

Peter followed his gaze and his own expression hardened. 'I see.'

'You're not really thinking about buying, are you?' Abby asked later, to break the silence as they walked home.

'It depends.' Nick shrugged.

'On what?'

'On. . .someone else.'

'Oh.'

Charlotte Canning. The dreamy enchantment that had held Abby as she explored the house splintered and shattered like glass. How could she have forgotten Charlotte Canning? Savage claws of jealousy tore at her heart as she thought of Nick living there with his beautiful co-star, and she lashed out in hurt.

'I hope you're not thinking of installing jacuzzis and swimming-pools!'

'No, and I wasn't wondering where to put the private cinema and hamburger bar either! No doubt you'd expect me to want those too?' There was an unfamiliar note of anger in Nick's voice.

'It wouldn't surprise me in the slightest,' Abby

snapped. 'But I'd hate to think of you ruining that lovely house.'

'Not nearly as much as you'd hate to admit that any of your prejudices were wrong!' His green eyes were steely as he looked down at her. 'You can find your own way home, Abigail. I'm going for a walk.'

Nick left the next day. Determined to show no interest in his affairs, Abby merely wished him a frigid goodbye when he explained that he was going to London to meet a friend and refused to admit to herself how much she missed him.

Instead she threw herself into her work, spending long hours in the studio hunched over the easel as the stack of pictures waiting to be cleaned steadily diminished. Rather regretfully she handed over the painting of Stynch Manor to its owner, a dealer who was delighted with the result.

'It's turned out to be quite a nice little picture, hasn't it? I won't have any trouble shifting it!'

Abby winced. She would like it to have gone to someone to whom Stynch Manor meant something. Instead it would be sold to some passing motorist who would hang it on a wall where it would stay, undusted and unappreciated, until it was obscured by another layer of grime.

The soothing routine of the studio had its inevitable effect, and gradually Abby regained her equilibrium. Looking back, it seemed as if she had been on a roller-coaster of emotions ever since Nick arrived and Abby found herself wondering how she could ever have behaved so uncharacteristically. She blamed the heat, the time of the month, Nick's resemblance to Stephen. The fact that Nick now chose to spend his time gallivanting with other women in London was neither here nor there to her. In future, she decided, she would be friendly, but distant, and made a determined effort not to look up whenever she heard a car turn into the lane, or to notice how quiet the cottage felt without him.

Nick reappeared a few days before he was due to open the church fête, and just when Abby was beginning to think that he was never going to return. She was padding round her bedroom getting ready for her evening shower when the purr of the Rolls-Royce sent her running to the window.

She was unprepared for the sickening jolt she felt when she realised that Nick was not alone. He was laughing as he helped his companion out of the car; even with her blonde hair now curling fashionably to her shoulders, Charlotte Canning was unmistakable in a cornflower-blue woollen dress that matched her eyes.

Instinctively Abby drew back from the open window, but the American actress's husky drawl was easily audible.

'Darling, how quaint!'

Nick's reply was muffled, but then they both laughed. To Abby, their laughter sounded mocking, hatefully reminiscent of those Washington parties, and her fingers curled. Peeking furtively round the curtain, she saw Nick put his arm round Charlotte and walk with her into the cottage. A moment later the front door closed softly behind them.

So it was true.

For a moment Abby could not move. She felt cold and sick, and then, in a glorious, heady rush, white fury, at herself, at Nick, but mostly at Charlotte

Canning. How dared she come here with her blonde hair and her perfect face and hateful, throaty laugh, simpering up at Nick as if she owned him? And that ridiculous outfit! Imagine wearing a clinging dress like that to the country—how tasteless! How vulgar! Abby looked down at her faded skirt and brown cardigan, darned and thin with age, and wanted to tear off Charlotte's dress and smack the perfect smile off her perfect face.

Abby spun on her heel away from the window and began to brush her hair with savage concentration. She could just imagine Nick and Charlotte next door, sneering at the 'quaint' ways of rural England, marvelling at the gawping locals, laughing at how easily Abigail Smith had succumbed to Nick's charms. . .

Anger buoyed her up all evening but the next morning when she awoke it was to a feeling of black, leaden despair. She shut herself in her studio and refused to think about Charlotte Canning next door with Nick. What were they doing? The curtains were still drawn. . .were they still asleep, curled up together, or waking to warm, slow kisses?

Stop it! Stop it! Stop it! Abby threw herself furiously into her work until Liz materialised in the doorway.

'So there you are! Nick told me I'd find you down here,' Liz said gaily. Abby's eyes narrowed. She would have thought Nick would have had other things on his mind than her whereabouts! 'Lucky I saw him, actually,' Liz went on. 'I was able to remind him about opening the fête.'

'He's got better things to do now,' Abby said with bitterness. 'Charlotte Canning has come to stay.'

'I know, he told me. We're getting quite blasé about

stars in Stynch Magna now, aren't we?' Liz beamed at
Abby. 'Nick said he was driving her back to London
today, but he promised faithfully he'd be back for the
fête. It's on Saturday, so he'll have to be quick!'

There were some fears that the good weather would
break at the weekend, but in the event the early
morning mists which threatened on the Saturday morning soon evaporated under the heat of another burning
day. The entire village seemed to buzz with activity as
Abby walked up to Stynch Manor, remembering her
last visit with Nick. She had loved the house so much;
now its air of desolation matched her own. Nick and
Charlotte had left two days ago, but the green Rolls-
Royce had still not returned. What if he never came
back? her heart whispered.

The empty windows looked out over a bustling scene
as card tables were pressed into service as stalls, cakes
delivered, microphones tested and the morris dancing
group had a last-minute rehearsal. Abby was in great
demand to draw original signs, until she was dragged
away by Liz and delegated, rather unwillingly, to the
'Guess the Doll's Name' stall.

'It's easy,' Liz explained briskly. 'Just get people to
write their guess on a bit of paper—after they've paid
their money of course!—and keep any that guess
correctly.'

'What is her name, though?' Abby asked, eyeing
the large, elaborately dressed doll doubtfully. It had
long golden hair, a blank blue stare and a prim rosebud
mouth.

'That's up to you. Call her whatever you like—
nobody else is going to know, after all. We'll announce
the winners at the end of the day.'

Abby picked up the doll and held it at arm's length. It had the kind of superficial looks that would appeal to Nick Carleton, she thought. Choosing a name was not hard.

'Her name's Charlotte.'

Anticipating a long, hot afternoon, she wore a cool dress in her favourite blues and greens. It fell in loose folds to the grass as she sat behind the card table which functioned as the stall, her chin propped in her hands, and surveyed the activity below her. Usually she enjoyed the fête, but this year she felt remote from it all. It was as if she were wrapped in a film of dreary greyness.

Even as she frowned at the thought, Nick strolled in through the gates, and the colour snapped back into the scene. Abby felt as if someone had reached out to squeeze her heart tight. He was here. His cream trousers and dark khaki shirt were unexpectedly sober, but there was something in his smile, and in his dark, exciting looks, that automatically drew the eye. He looked relaxed and tanned as he chatted easily with the crowds.

Abby realised that she was staring hungrily at him and caught herself up. He might seem to be alone, but that didn't mean Charlotte Canning wasn't curled up in bed, or drumming her perfectly manicured nails impatiently for his return. Abby pursed her lips and looked instead at the queues forming up to pay their entrance fee. She had never seen so many people at the fête before.

'They're all coming to see Nick Carleton open the fête,' the vicar's wife explained as she issued Abby with a small amount of change. 'Robert was rather nervous about asking him to do it, but he couldn't have been nicer. Such a charming man! But of course you must know that, being his neighbour.' She put her head on one side and looked expectantly at Abby. News of their visit to Chez Florimonde and holding hands in the pub would not have escaped Mrs Bolton.

'He can certainly be very pleasant when he wants to.' Abby kept her voice deliberately cool.

Mrs Bolton leant over confidentially. 'Between you and me, dear, Nick Carleton has already been more than generous. He told Robert that he'd been to visit the church, and gave him a *huge* cheque to put towards the restoration of the spire. Robert was quite overwhelmed. What with that, and attracting all the crowds today, Nick really has saved our church. Wasn't it generous of him?'

'I expect he can afford it,' Abby said ungraciously.

The older woman was taken aback. 'Well, even so, dear. . .It can't be very nice with people never leaving you in peace, always wanting you to *do* something for them—sign an autograph, open a fête, buy a raffle ticket. . .'

Abby glanced over to where Nick was standing in a mob of young fans, signing autographs, and reducing the girls to giggles. He looked, suddenly, lean and dangerous, a tiger surrounded by rabbits.

Without warning, he looked up and Abby found herself staring directly into his eyes over the heads of his adoring entourage. He was some distance away, but they might have been standing mere inches apart. Abby had the uncomfortable feeling that he could read her mind, and with a physical effort she wrenched her eyes away.

'I think Robert wants to open the fête now,' said Mrs Bolton, who had caught sight of the vicar hovering ineffectually near Nick. 'We won't be able to hold everyone back much longer.' She set off purposefully to organise her husband. 'Come along, dear.'

Drawn unwillingly along in Mrs Bolton's wake, Abby found herself part of a large crowd which had gathered around a raised platform. The vicar was clearing his throat self-consciously and the microphone crackled and then gave a long whine as if to announce that it was ready. He kept his speech mercifully short as he introduced Nick, who leapt lightly on to the platform to a storm of clapping.

'Slimy sort of fellow, isn't he?' said a voice in Abby's ear, and she turned her head sharply to find Peter Middleton standing next to her.

'What do you mean?'

'This Carleton chap.' Peter jerked his head at the platform where Nick was in the middle of a story that set the laughter rippling through the crowd. 'I wouldn't trust him further than I could throw him. What on earth do you see in him?' Peter's face was sullen.

'Nick is *not* slimy!' Abby whispered furiously without thinking.

'Of course he is. Look at him! He turns all that American charm on and off like a tap. He just fancies himself as the English squire at the moment—it's a new role for him.'

Nick was coming to the end of his speech. 'Finally, I'd like to take this opportunity of thanking you all for making me so welcome here in your village.' Was it her imagination, or did his eyes flicker to Abby for a brief moment? 'I guess it sounds kind of odd for an

American to be saying this, but I envy you your
traditions here. I haven't been here long, but I have
been to visit your church. I find it incredible that it's
stood here for—what? Seven, eight hundred years?
And for all that time there have been people just like
you living here, taking the church for granted as the
focal point of the community. It's a symbol of conti-
nuity with your past. Don't let it fall apart now. I'm
going to urge you to spend as much as you can at the
fête today—and I'll match every penny you give for
the church restoration fund.' There was a rustle of
surprise at this, but Nick held up his hand. 'We're
wasting good spending time as it is, so I now officially
declare the fête open. I've only one last thing to say—
which I know you'll all expect of me—and
that's. . .Have a nice day now!'

There was a pause after he had finished, and then
the crowd erupted into loud applause, before breaking
up to filter away to the stalls.

Abby was glad to be kept busy all afternoon—
anything to keep her mind off Nick. Her confused
whirl of emotions at seeing him again had settled into
a simmering anger at herself for wasting so much time
thinking about a man who was everything she disliked
most. She resented the way her heart leapt to see him,
resented the long hours of wretchedness and the sick
jealousy of a woman she had never met and could
never, ever, hope to rival. It was high time she pulled
herself together!

From her vantage-point she could see Liz doing
brisk business selling raffle tickets. As her friend had
predicted, it seemed as if every female in the village
wanted a chance to win a kiss from Nick Carleton.

That was one stall she *wouldn't* be patronising, Abby decided firmly. If Nick wanted to indulge the fantasies of silly girls, that was up to him. She couldn't care less *who* won first prize. She wondered if Charlotte Canning knew that Nick was up for sale this afternoon.

It was impossible not to be aware of Nick himself, who was making a point of visiting every stall except hers. Abby could see him moving from stall to stall, pausing to shake hands and joke with people as he went. It was a wonder they weren't all tugging their forelocks, she thought acidly, remembering Peter's comment about Nick playing the squire.

'Miss! Is she called Rosamund?'

Recalled to her duties, Abby turned back to her small customer, and when she looked up again Nick seemed to have disappeared.

The afternoon wore on. At half-past four there was a marked lull in the activity. Everyone seemed to have taken a break for tea, and a languid silence had settled over the fête. Abby leant on the table and surveyed Stynch Manor with half-closed eyes, allowing herself to imagine it repainted and refurbished. There would be curtains hanging at the windows, the front door would be open to the sun, she would be pruning the roses, a dark green Rolls-Royce would arrive crunching on fresh gravel and——

'Hi, there!'

Abby started violently, knocking a pile of coins on to the grass at her feet. 'Nick!' Without thinking she jumped to her feet, shaken by a gust of emotions at seeing him so close. They stared at each other in taut silence, then Abby crouched down to gather up the scattered coins. 'What did you creep up on me like that for?' she demanded, furious at the quaver in her voice, and desperate in case he had seen the first, heart-stopping moment of joy in her eyes.

'I didn't creep up on you.' The odd expression in Nick's eyes faded into amusement. 'You were miles away. You had a real dreamy look about you.' What were you dreaming about, Abigail?'

Something in his voice made Abby look up swiftly and for a wild moment she was tempted to tell him. But the memory of Charlotte Canning shimmered before her, and in the end her eyes dropped and she resumed her search. 'Oh, nothing.'

'Must have been a nice nothing.' As she stood up, he picked up a coin from the grass at his feet. 'Here, you missed this one.' He handed it gravely to Abby who snatched it out of his hand with bad grace.

'Excuse me.' Blushing furiously, a girl of fifteen or so hovered beside them. She was a lumpy girl, with a plain face and heavy spectacles, but Nick smiled at her as if she were Charlotte Canning herself.

'Hi,' he said easily. 'What can we do for you?'

'Well, I. . .if you wouldn't mind. . .that is, I've got this picture. . .' She floundered around in a morass of sentences, and in the end simply held out a tattered photo of Nick.

'Do you want me to sign it?' he asked kindly, and she nodded mutely. 'Gee, I hate this shot—it makes me look as if I've got false teeth!'

He showed it to Abby who gave it a cursory glance. 'Ghastly,' she agreed, determined not to succumb to his charm.

The girl looked on in astonishment. 'I th-think it's great!'

Nick twinkled at her. 'Thanks, honey. There should be more people like you around. Now, what's your name?'

'Elaine.'

'Elaine, right.' Taking a pen out of his breast pocket, he wrote, 'To Elaine, with very best wishes on a beautiful summer's day,' and then signed it. Abby noticed that his writing was angular and very neat. She would have expected a flourish to be more his style.

Scarlet with pleasure, Elaine took the photo back as if it were a holy relic. 'Thank you,' she stammered. 'I'm sorry to have disturbed you.'

'Not at all.' Nick shook her hand warmly. 'It's been a pleasure to meet you.'

As Elaine stumbled away, hugging the photograph to her, Abby said, 'You love all this, don't you?'

'All what?'

'All the attention.' She waved her hand after Elaine. 'All the adoration.'

Nick turned towards her. 'Yes,' he said slowly, 'yes, I do like the attention. I like people. I like people to like me. But adoration—no, not really. Elaine's just a kid, all kids have a crush on someone. They love the image, not the real person.' He gave a self-deprecating smile. 'I doubt if she'd still adore me if she really knew me.'

'She certainly wouldn't if she had to put up with your awful whistling!' Abby plonked herself down at the table and began stacking the coins in neat piles.

Nick stood looking down at her. 'Why do you find it so difficult to like me, Abigail Smith?' Abby went on grimly counting coins. 'I've tried harder with you than anyone. Hell, I even put away my loud shirts for you.

I put on this boring shirt especially for you, and you haven't even noticed it.'

'It's certainly a great improvement,' Abby said coldly, refusing to give in to the cajoling note in his voice. She wasn't going to be taken in again.

Suddenly he placed both hands on the card table and leant down so that his face was close to hers. 'You've been avoiding me,' he stated flatly.

Abby's hands stilled. 'I thought *you* had been avoiding *me*,' she retorted, meeting his eyes bravely. She had forgotten just how green they were.

'Me?' To her relief he pushed himself upright once more. 'I haven't been avoiding you. Whenever I've tried to see you, you've shut yourself in that damned studio of yours.'

'*I* haven't been away in London for the last three weeks!' Abby said before she could stop herself, glad of the new rush of anger. 'If you'd wanted to see me, you knew where to find me. I've been sitting here all afternoon,' she swept on, 'but you've been everywhere except here. Don't talk to me about avoiding *you*!'

'I haven't exactly been free to do what I want. I did my duty having a go at all the stalls, and I was just on my way to you when I got dragged off to judge the home-grown produce competition. I didn't realise so much diplomacy was required in judging zucchini! I've had a go at the lucky dip, inspected the jumble stall, bought three cakes and a jar of rhubarb chutney, and now I'm free to not avoid you.' His voice dropped. 'I've missed you, Abby.'

So he'd missed her, had he? So much that he spent all his time in London with Charlotte Canning? Abby's eyes glittered dangerously. She could still hear Charlotte drawling, 'How quaint!' followed by their mocking laughter.

'Really?' she said in a voice that dripped ice. 'Perhaps you'd like to have a go at this stall now, since you've been such a martyr to the cause.' She thrust the doll into his hands. 'If you guess her name correctly, you get to take her home. A beautiful doll like that ought to appeal to you, Nick!'

CHAPTER EIGHT

Nick turned the doll in his hands consideringly. 'Now why would you think something like that, Abigail Smith?' he mused, without taking his eyes from its face.

'Your girlfriends are hardly noted for their brain-power, are they?' she replied nastily.

'Which girlfriends, Abby?'

Abby hesitated. Although he was still contemplating the doll with apparent calmness, she sensed a simmering anger. But it was too late to turn back now, and anyway, why should she spare *his* feelings? 'Charlotte Canning, for instance.'

'Charlotte?' She had been right about the anger. He stared at her now with glacial eyes. 'One, Charlotte is a very bright lady indeed. She's certainly a lot brighter than you are, Abigail, though I guess you'd never be prepared to admit it. And two, she is not one of my girlfriends.'

'Come off it, Nick! She spent the night at your cottage. I saw her with my own eyes.'

'And your prim little English mind put two and two together and made six and a half, right? Ever heard of such a thing as platonic friendship, Abigail?'

'Platonic wasn't the word I'd use to describe the way you two were. . .pawing. . .each other!' Abby snapped, as angry as Nick now.

Nick bared his teeth in a ferocious smile. 'Don't tell me you were spying on us?'

'No, I was not! It was difficult to avoid seeing you. I can assure you I've got better things to do than watch you fondling in public!'

'Why don't you do them, then?' Nick thrust his face close to hers and instinctively Abby stepped back from the implacable hardness in his eyes. 'I'm sick of you, Abigail. You're so wrapped up in your prejudices, you can't see what's in front of your nose. I'll bet you think you're brighter than all these people here, just like you think you're brighter than Charlotte. You may have seen more of the world than they have, but it's made you more narrow minded, not less. They've all accepted me as I am, but not Abigail Smith. Oh, no! Abigail knows all about Americans, Abigail's not going to make the effort to welcome a stranger.

'I've been touched by the generosity of people here, but you're not from here, and it shows. You're mean with yourself Abigail—at best you're a tease. No wonder Peter found you hard to make out. Did you lead him on like you led me on?'

Abby's grey eyes were huge in her white face. 'I didn't lead you on!' she whispered.

'Didn't you? It sure felt like it!' She held up a hand as if in protest, but Nick was unmoved. 'Don't look at me with those big grey eyes—I'm not falling for that any more. You're cold, Abby. I don't think you're capable of falling in love,—you're too wrapped up in yourself. Well, you can keep your prissy tied-up hair and your cat and your garden. Go ahead and be a dried-up old spinster—it's all you deserve!

'Here, take this!' He shoved the doll back at her. 'I

don't need any plastic dolls. I'm only interested in real, warm, living women—and that excludes you!'

Turning on his heel, Nick strode off towards the house, leaving Abby staring blankly down at the doll, her eyes stinging with unshed tears. No one had ever spoken to her so contemptuously before, not even Stephen. Never had she imagined that Nick could be so bitterly angry.

Cold. Narrow-minded. Prissy. Prim. Mean. Prejudiced.

Was that really how he saw her? Was that really how she was? Abby began to shake as she remembered the look in Nick's eyes and her mouth trembled. Determinedly she bit down on her lower lip. She wouldn't cry. She *wouldn't*.

For the rest of the afternoon Abby sat miserably by her table, longing for the day to end. A cold stone of misery sat heavy on her stomach as Nick's words circled in an endless echo round her brain. Cold. Narrow-minded. Prissy. Prim. Mean. Prejudiced. He was right; she had indulged her bitterness about Stephen for far too long. Looking back, Stephen's features seemed blurry now. How could she have compared him with Nick?

Her eyes rested on Nick, who gave no sign that he had been involved in a bitter quarrel. He was handing out rosettes at the pet show, laughingly fending off the paws of an exuberant dog. It must seem poor entertainment compared to Hollywood. He could be amusing himself anywhere he wanted; instead he was here in this very ordinary village, devoting himself to making people feel special, and never by so much as a flicker letting them imagine that he wasn't enjoying himself too. And yet. . .he *was* enjoying himself, that was obvious.

Abby's stomach twisted. She had been so stupid!

'Are you OK, Abby?' Liz was looking down at her with concern. 'You look a bit peculiar.'

'I'm fine.' With an effort Abby summoned a smile. 'A bit of a headache, that's all. Must be all the excitement!'

'Well, we're finishing up now. Nick's about to present the prizes. Do you want to bring the doll down now and hand over your takings?'

Together they walked down to where Mrs Bolton was organising the prizes. 'My dears, thank you so much for all your help. We've had record takings, thanks to Nick Carleton—and we haven't finished counting yet!'

'Come on, let's go and watch Nick hand out the prizes,' said Liz.

Abby found herself in the middle of a large crowd, all talking and laughing good-naturedly in the late afternoon sunshine. Nick was on the platform making the first presentations. There were claps and wolf-whistles as a stout woman clambered up to receive a bottle of wine and a kiss on the cheek from Nick. Bridling with pleasure, she resumed her place to the accompaniment of envious looks from her companions.

The vicar's voice crackled over the microphone, announcing the name of the next winner, and Abby found her attention wandering back to Nick. She stared at him as if she had never seen him before. He stood easily on the platform, towering over the vicar, and cracking jokes as each new prize-winner climbed up the steps. The dark shirt suited him, she decided. It made him look older—or was it something in his face?

Suddenly there was a rustle of expectant excitement and Abby dragged her attention back to the vicar. '. . .and now for the last prize, the one all the ladies have been waiting for, I know. We'll now find out who has won first prize in the raffle, which is a kiss from Nick himself. The lucky lady is. . .' He opened a slip of paper and beamed over his spectacles at the crowd. 'Abby Smith!'

Beside her, Abby heard Liz squeak with delight and there was much good-humoured jostling while she stood as if turned to stone. This couldn't be happening!

'Go on, Abby,' Liz urged, giving her a little push.

'But. . .I didn't buy a ticket!' Abby whispered urgently.

'I bought one for you.'

'You *what*?'

'I knew you wouldn't buy one yourself,' Liz said innocently, adding quickly, 'Look, Peter's green with jealousy.'

'But. . .' Abby's protests were lost as the crowd urged her forwards and somehow she found herself standing on the platform next to Nick. Scarlet with embarrassment, she was conscious only of him as the claps and wolf-whistles gained in volume.

'I didn't buy a ticket,' she muttered.

'I'm quite sure you didn't.' Nick came towards her, his smile rather hard. 'But you seem to have won a kiss anyway. What would you like, a nice frigid peck on the cheek?'

Abby's eyes stung with tears. He hadn't forgiven her. If only this were all over! She nodded mutely.

'Well, that's too bad. We don't want to disappoint our audience, do we?' Nick reached out and pulled her towards him, one hand hard in the small of her back, the other forcing her chin up to look at him.

The crowd fell silent as they stared at each other. His eyes were jewel-bright with suppressed anger and Abby tried to pull away, but he was too strong for her. With a smothered exclamation, he jerked her closer and swooped to capture her mouth in a fierce kiss.

His lips were hard and cruel. Abby struggled at first, until the hand under her chin slid round to the nape of her neck, holding her as if in a vice, while the other pressed her against the hard line of his body. And then, imperceptibly, the quality of his kiss changed. Abby could feel his anger dissolve, even as her own struggles were swamped by a sweet tide of response. His grip on her relaxed, his hand sliding down her back. Abby's own hands were still rammed against his chest, but there were no thoughts of pushing him away as her fingers curled against the material of his shirt.

He was so strong, so solid. His mouth was so warm now, as if those first fierce moments had never been. Abby was enveloped in hazy delight; she never knew how long she stood there, locked in his arms, oblivious to the cheering crowds. Nothing mattered but his kiss.

At length, Nick's hold slackened, and he released her slowly. Abby stared up at him with huge dark eyes, as if in a daze, her whole body aching with the need to feel his arms around her again. Nick's expression was unreadable.

The vicar cleared his throat. 'Well, I'm sure Abby

won't forget her prize in a hurry. I'm afraid that marks the end of the fête for this year. It only remains for me to thank Nick Carleton once again, and, of course, all of you, for coming along and supporting the church. I hope we will see you all again next year.'

Desultory clapping marked the end of his speech, and gradually the crowds began to drift away through the gates. Abby felt herself the object of many speculative and envious glances as she stumbled off the platform.

'Bet it was rigged,' someone murmured.

'Funny how the best-looking girl won the kiss,' Sarah remarked loudly to her boyfriend, who looked glumly after Abigail.

'Can't say I blame him.'

Ignoring all the nods and winks, she fled back to dismantle her stall. Her face burned. How could Nick have kissed her like that in front of everyone? How could she have responded so eagerly? He could have pushed her down and made love to her there and then and she would only have begged for more!

'You've made a fine fool of yourself now, haven't you?' Peter Middleton's words echoed her thoughts so exactly that she flinched as if she had been slapped.

Peter's face was bitter as he watched her unpin the sign and begin folding up the legs of the card table. Abby wished he would go away.

'What do you mean?' she asked dully.

'Letting yourself be mauled in public like that! I wouldn't have thought it of you, Abby. You always seemed so mature and sensible, the last person to have her head turned by a handsome face.'

'I haven't had my head turned!' Abby snapped the last leg into place.

'Oh, come on, Abby!' Peter gave a short laugh. 'You could hardly keep your eyes off him when we looked round the house. I'm not blind. And we all saw the way you looked at him after he kissed you just now. You had longing written all over your face. I never realised you wanted a man so much. I always thought you weren't interested in sex. You certainly never wanted me. I wasn't good enough for you, was I? Were you waiting for someone rich to come along, or did you just want a hunk? That's all Nick Carleton is after all—a rich hunk!'

Abby's fists clenched, but she forced herself to stay calm. 'I think you've said enough.'

'He doesn't love you, you know.'

'I know,' she said quietly.

'He's just a pretty face. He'll only ever love himself.'

Wasn't that what Nick had said about her? 'You're wrong,' said Abby. 'There's more to Nick than you could ever guess at, Peter.'

Peter snorted. 'I'm disappointed in you, Abby. I always thought of you as a woman of discernment.'

Abby's smile was bitter. 'I always thought that too.' Out of the corner of her eye she could see Nick shaking hands with the vicar. He flexed his shoulders wearily and began to make his way along the drive back to the road. The crowds had gone, and he walked alone, head bent, hands thrust deep into his pockets.

He looks tired, she thought, and a wave of tenderness swept over her. She wanted to rush home and make him comfortable, to smooth away the lines of tiredness from his face with her fingers. . .

'. . .up to you!' Peter's voice broke into her thoughts.

'What was that?' she asked.

'I *said*, if you want to make a fool of yourself over Nick Carleton, it's up to you!'

Abby's eyes rested on Nick's receding figure. Suddenly everything seemed very clear. 'Yes,' she agreed. 'It is.'

How could she have been so blind? How could she have fallen so hopelessly in love without realising it?

Abby walked slowly home, thinking of how Nick had swept into her life, shaking up her preconceptions and stirring emotions she had not known she had possessed. She had tried hard to resist him, had clung to her memories of past bitterness, but he had laid waste to all her defences and there was nothing left for her now but to admit defeat.

And to apologise. Dismally Abby remembered how quick she had been to judge him. The least she could do now was to tell Nick she was sorry. She owed him that.

Suddenly it seemed vitally important to see Nick and explain. She quickened her pace, was almost running by the time she turned into the lane. But there was only an empty space where the big green car usually stood.

He had gone.

Abby's shoulders slumped in despair and she stood quite still staring at the empty verge, as if willing the car to reappear. Nick must have driven straight back to Charlotte Canning. The thought tore at her heart.

Well, what had she expected? Why would he wait to

say goodbye to her, when all she had done was show herself to be stupidly prejudiced? *Cold. Prissy. Prim. Mean.* The tears trickled down her cheeks unheeded as she let herself into the cottage. Elijah ran to welcome her, and she picked him up, hugging him close for comfort. Despite the heavy heat of the afternoon, he seemed the only warmth in a cold and cheerless world.

Later that night she lay on her bed dully watching the moonlight shadows wavering on the ceiling. The air was oppressively hot and sticky and she had opened her window wide in the hope of catching any breeze. She tried not to imagine Nick and Charlotte Canning together, and longed only for Nick to come home so that she could at least see him again. If only he came alone. . .

It was past midnight when the Rolls returned. Abby tensed, waiting to hear the murmur of voices, but there was only a soft click as Nick closed the car door. She could hear the creak of the garden gate and the sound of the key in the front door. Then there was nothing until a thud and the muffled sound of swearing.

He must be creeping around in the dark, she thought to herself with a smile. The thought was inexpressibly comforting. He was alone, that was all that mattered. In the morning she would see him and apologise. She began rehearsing what she would say, but fell asleep at last in mid-sentence.

In the morning it did not seem quite so simple. Abby's stomach churned at the thought of facing Nick. Was it only yesterday that he had kissed her so bitterly in front of all those people? It seemed as if months had passed since she had admitted to herself how much she loved him.

She stood under the shower for long minutes, then dithered over what to wear. She yearned to see Nick, but dreaded what he would say. In the end she chose a soft skirt in mingled golds and browns, with a plain top, and brushed her hair until it shone. With a mouth full of grips, she held the hair away from her face and began to pin it up as normal in front of the mirror, trying to avoid thinking about Nick.

When she had finished, she inspected her reflection anxiously. Somehow she had imagined that her new feelings for Nick would show in her face, that she would look different in some way. But, apart from a smoky tinge in her grey eyes, she looked just as normal. On an impulse, Abby reached up and pulled out the grips in her hair, shaking the silky chestnut tresses about her face.

She peered through them at the mirror, hit by a sudden wave of aching despair. It would take more than a new hairstyle to turn her into a glamorous blonde.

Turning away from her reflection, she walked resolutely downstairs and opened the back door. Even if she could never compete with Charlotte Canning, she could still apologise.

Outside the air was as close as the previous night. Ever hopeful of breakfast, Elijah materialised at her feet, and Abby bent to stroke him, glad of the diversion.

'Keep your paws crossed for me, puss.' She straightened up only to find Nick watching her silently from the other side of the gate. Shock drove the breath from her body and when he said, 'Hi,' quietly, she could only manage a strangled 'Hello' in return. He seemed to stand out in vivid relief against the familiar background which faded until there were only the two of them looking at each other.

He looked tired still and unusually serious, but the green eyes were as bright as ever. At the sight of him, all Abby's fine speeches were forgotten. She could do no more than stare back at him, separated only by the wooden gate and the tabby weaving unnoticed around her legs.

The silence stretched, became unbearable. Abby licked lips which were suddenly dry.

'Nick——' she began.

'Look——' Nick said at the same time, and they both stopped awkwardly.

'I just wanted——' she started again, just as he tried,

'Abby, I——'

This time they laughed.

'Ladies first!' Nick offered.

Now that the moment had come, Abby could find nothing to say. Nick unlatched the gate and came to stand before her, his eyes questioning.

'You usually jump over.' She said, stupidly, the first thing that came into her mind.

Nick smiled in a way that made her heart begin to pound slowly and painfully. 'You usually wear your hair up.' He reached out to touch it lightly. 'It's beautiful like that.'

'Nick.' Abby took a deep breath and suddenly it did not seem so difficult after all. 'I just wanted to say I was sorry for the way I've behaved.' He opened his mouth to speak, but she hurried on, 'I deserved everything you said to me yesterday. I've been stupid and prejudiced, like you said, and——' She paused, searching for the right words, before giving a helpless shrug. 'There isn't really anything to say, except I'm sorry. I wish I could do something to change your opinion of me.'

Nick looked at her. He didn't smile but there was a light in his eyes that lit a spark of hope in her heart. 'I'm never going to change my opinion of you, Abigail,' he said firmly, but when he saw the dismay flicker in her face, reached out and pulled her to him in a tight hug, so tight that she could feel the warm beat of his heart close to hers. 'I think you're beautiful,' he murmured against her hair, and now she could feel him smile. 'I'm just not prepared to change my mind about that!'

Dazzling relief flooded through Abby. She pulled away from him slightly to look up at his face as he went on. 'Don't you want to know what I wanted to say to you?' She nodded mutely. 'I wanted to say that I was sorry too. Those things I said to you were unforgivable. I didn't mean any of them, Abby, you must know that,' he said, his voice urgent. 'I was just so happy to see you again, and then you were so cold. . .' He paused. 'Hell, I don't know what happened. I just lost my head. I guess I wanted to hurt you the same way I felt you'd hurt me. I deliberately humiliated you in front of all those people. When I left the fête yesterday, I was so angry I got straight in the car to drive to London, but as soon as I got there I turned round and came back to tell you that I was sorry.'

With a last quick squeeze, he released her. 'Look, let's start again. What say we go out for the day somewhere, just the two of us? I've got a script to read, and you can bring your sketch-book.'

'Where were you thinking of going?' Abby asked cautiously, uncertain of how to react. There was no mention of Charlotte, but perhaps Nick as a friend was better than no Nick at all.

'Anywhere.' Nick gestured expansively. 'We could just follow the stream, see where it goes. Come on, Abby,' he coaxed. 'I'll even provide a picnic lunch.'

Abby hesitated, then relented. The temptation of spending a whole day with Nick was too hard to resist. 'As long as it's not peanut butter and jelly sandwiches!'

They set off an hour later, with a shabby tartan rug and lunch packed in a wicker basket. At the cattlegrid they paused to inspect the escape route they had made. The plank was still in place and there was no sign of the frogs except for a few pitiful corpses.

'They're either dead or sitting very, very still,' Nick commented, peering down into the depths. He grinned down at Abby. 'Would you like me to carry you across?'

She shook her head, embarrassed at having confided so childish a fear, but was glad when he took her hand and helped her across. Breathing a sigh of relief, she smiled up at him. 'Thanks.'

His grip on her hand tightened. Abruptly he said, 'Charlotte really is just a friend, Abby.'

'Oh.'

Although no more was said, it was enough to set the seal on a day of unalloyed happiness for Abby. The fields were awash with wild flowers, the bright primary colours of poppies and cowslips and daisies, as they walked through the long grass down to the stream, and followed its path, ducking beneath overhanging branches or taking off their shoes to splash through the cool water whenever the track disappeared into undergrowth.

At length they reached a patch of meadow, sheltered by a wood on one side. Far from any sign of civilisation, they were alone with the trees and the long, sweet grass and the sky.

Nick threw himself on to the rug and lay propped on one elbow, reading a script and absently chewing a blade of grass, while Abby sat a little way away on a folding stool, sketch-book on her knees. Black storm clouds were massing in the distance. She tried to concentrate on capturing their looming presence behind the drowsy peacefulness of the scene, but her attention kept wandering back to Nick, to the lean, hard strength of him as he lay stretched out, a line of concentration between his eyes.

'Is the script any good?' she asked eventually.

'Nope. Lousy.' He tossed it aside and lay back, his hands under his head. 'I guess I'll just have to lie here and look at the sky instead. How are you doing?'

'Lousy,' Abby imitated him, and he grinned. 'I can't get that pre-storm light.'

'Come and sit down here. It's too hot to be creative.'

Nick patted the rug beside him and she went to join him, clasping her hands lightly round her knees. 'Those clouds are really building up now. I think we're in for quite a storm. You can feel it in the air.' She glanced down at him. 'Do you think we ought to head for home?'

'Do you want to go home?' Nick countered.

'No.'

'Nor do I.'

Abby glanced at him again, and this time she could not look away.

Nick reached out and took her hand. 'I really am sorry about the things I said to you yesterday, Abby.'

'Don't be. You were quite right.' She tore her eyes away from his and looked once more at the massing clouds. 'I've spent too long feeling bitter about Stephen and what happened in the States. I told you that he dropped me when he thought I was no more use to him as a contact with my stepfather. What I didn't tell you is that I found out I was pregnant almost the next day. I was absolutely terrified, but Stephen wouldn't answer any of my calls. He had one of those awful telephone answering machines. All I ever got was his voice saying that he was sorry, he was not available—as if I didn't know!

'After a while I began to cling to the thought of the baby. Maybe I thought it would bring Stephen back to me eventually, maybe it just seemed as if it would be a sort of security for me. I don't know.' Abby sighed. 'Anyway, a couple of months later, when I'd given up phoning, I came face to face with Stephen in the street. He had another woman with him and he looked straight through me as if I didn't exist, had never existed. It was just such a shock seeing him again. I was so desperate, I just turned away. I didn't look where I was going, and stepped in front of a car.'

Seeing Nick's expression, she said quickly, 'It was my own stupid fault. It was nothing to do with Stephen. I just. . .didn't look, that's all.' She fell silent, remembering the screaming brakes, the whirling darkness, the pain of waking up in hospital.

'Did you lose the baby, Abby?' Nick asked gently.

She nodded. 'They kept telling me I was lucky to be alive, but for a long time it didn't feel like it. I lay in that hospital bed in a sort of black despair and thought about losing Stephen and the baby, and I blamed America because it was easier than blaming myself. I was the one who got pregnant, I was the one who stepped in front of the car. But when you arrived, it was as if you were bringing America with you, so then I blamed you for all the bitterness just because you had an American accent.'

'I can understand why you'd feel bitter, Abby,' said Nick. 'No wonder you didn't want an American moving in next door.'

'It's the only reason I was resistant to your legendary charm,' Abby said in an attempt to lighten the conversation.

'Was?' he queried, taking her cue.

Abby didn't answer, but they smiled at each other in a wordless understanding that set happiness beating insistently somewhere deep inside her, and when Nick finally looked away it was if they had shared a long conversation.

'I have a confession to make,' he said, reaching over for the picnic basket.

'Oh?' Abby lay back on the rug and closed her eyes against the sun. She felt as if she had slipped a great burden from her shoulders.

'You know how the shops are closed here on a Sunday?'

'Yes.' She opened one eye, wondering where all this was leading.

'Well, it turned out that I didn't really have very much in the kitchen to make lunch with. . .' He handed her a small, foil-wrapped package which she opened with resignation.

'Not peanut butter!'

'I left out the jelly,' Nick offered, with the air of one making a great sacrifice, so that Abby laughed. 'And,' he went on, 'to help them slip down a bit easier, I managed to find a bottle of champagne!' He produced it with a flourish, twisting the cork out expertly, and pouring the sparkling liquid into two plastic mugs.

'Here's to transatlantic understanding,' he toasted her and they chinked mugs.

Abby chewed her way valiantly through one of the sandwiches, then thankfully gave the other to Nick, who wolfed it down. 'They're much better with jelly,' he assured her.

'I'll stick to the champagne, thanks.' She leant back with a contented sigh and closed her eyes once more. 'This is heaven.' The summer scent of grass was as intoxicating as the champagne and she breathed in deeply.

'Abigail.'

She opened her eyes to find Nick leaning over her. Behind his head the sky was very dark, and the first faint stirrings of breeze rustled in the branches of the trees near by, but Abby was aware only of the deep, mesmerising green of his eyes and the hazy excitement of his nearness.

Unthinkingly, she lifted a hand to touch his hair.

'Abigail,' Nick said again, as if savouring the word in his mouth, and smiled.

And because it seemed the natural thing to do, Abby smiled back up at him and moved her hands so that they rested on either side of his neck. His pulse was strong and steady beneath the warm skin, as she rubbed her thumbs almost thoughtfully over the masculine roughness of his jaw.

Very carefully, Nick stroked away a wayward strand of hair from her face. In the distance, thunder rumbled ominously, but neither heard it as he lowered his head and their lips met at last in a kiss which lit a deep glow within her, sending the blood in a tingling surge through her veins.

'You're so beautiful, Abby,' Nick murmured against her skin, and she quivered as his mouth left hers to trace a path of exquisite delight along her jawline, drifting downwards to the pulse beating wildly in the shadow of her throat. 'I've wanted you for so long.'

Arching her neck, Abby shivered at the naked desire in his deep voice. Her own fingers were at the buttons of his shirt, while Nick's hand drifted in impatient exploration over the curves of her body. Reaching one slim knee, he slid his hand possessively upwards under her skirt and along the silken length of her thigh, making Abby gasp at the insistent pleasure of his strong fingers.

'Nick!' His shirt was undone at last, leaving her free to slip her arms beneath the soft material, revelling in the satiny steel of his muscles beneath her fingers.

A first warning drop of rain fell heavily on to the bare skin of her leg, a second on her face.

Nick was playing her body like an instrument. Abby

strummed to his touch, tossing in restless anticipation as he brushed aside the thin cotton of her top and bent his head to explore the enticing curve of her breast with his lips.

'Lord, Abby, you feel so good,' he muttered hoarsely against her throat, his breathing ragged.

'Don't stop,' she whispered in his ear, pressing feverish kisses wherever she could, but at that moment the gathering darkness was split by a vicious tear of lightning, followed by the crack of thunder, and the heavens opened.

CHAPTER NINE

IT WAS as if a bucket had been emptied over their heads. In seconds they were soaked.

'Hell!' With a howl of frustration, Nick shook a fist and swore at the sky, his expression so outraged that Abby began to giggle. She lay back on her elbows, heedless of her dishevelled clothes, and laughed up at him.

'What kind of climate is this?' Nick had leapt to his feet and was frantically throwing the remains of the picnic back into the basket. He pulled her to her feet. 'It's not funny!' he protested, but was unable to prevent a grin at her helpless amusement. 'Of all the times. . .!'

Yanking her back into his arms, he kissed her again, and, careless of the pelting rain, Abby kissed him back. She could taste the rain on his face and feel the heat of his skin through the sodden material of his shirt. They might as well have been naked.

When thunder rumbled menacingly close again, Nick released her with reluctance. 'Come on, we'd better get home as soon as we can.'

Hand in hand and still laughing, they ran through the long grass. Abby was hampered by her skirt which clung to her legs, while Nick struggled to keep the wet blanket under his arm.

When they finally burst into the shelter of the cottage, both were drenched and gasping for breath.

Abby leant panting against the wall, a puddle of water forming at her feet. Her hair hung in rats' tails about her face and her skin glowed with exertion. A trickle of water ran down her neck and she wiped it away with her fingers before it disappeared into the shadowy cleft between her breasts. Looking up, she found Nick watching her and caught her breath at the light kindling in his eyes.

No words were spoken as he came towards her and placed his hands flat against the wall on either side of her. Instead, she wound her arms about his neck and pulled his head down, her own need as urgent as his. His kisses were rough, bruising her lips, but she sank into them, hungering for more.

'You've been under my skin all summer,' Nick murmured, pulling slightly away to look down into her flushed face. 'How did you do that, Abigail Smith?' His voice was very deep and warm.

Abby's lips drifted over the hard, exciting planes of his face, tasting him, savouring him, but at his question she paused, tilting back her head to look back at him with eyes that had deepened to a smoky purple. For a timeless moment they stared at each other until at last she spoke.

'Don't call me Abigail Smith,' was all she said, but Nick was not fooled by the full mouth that quivered irresistibly and opened eagerly to his as he gathered her close once more.

'Abby,' he conceded with a smile. With deft fingers, he unzipped her skirt and unpeeled it carefully from her rain-soaked skin. And then his hands were unbuttoning her camisole top until it too lay in a damp heap at her feet and she stood naked and golden before him.

At the feel of his fingers, so strong and sure, Abby shivered.

'Cold, Abby?' Nick murmured without ceasing his devastating assault on her senses.

'No,' she breathed, catching her breath in a sudden gasp as Nick's lips followed the trail of fire lit by his hands. 'No, not cold. Not cold at all.'

With that, Nick swept her into his arms and carried her upstairs to lay her down on the bed. His own clothes were quickly discarded and she welcomed him into her arms, glorying in the spiralling sensation of skin upon skin.

Mumbling endearments, Nick slid his hands over her body, discovering every secret dip and curve as his lips travelled over the honey-coloured warmth while Abby explored his compact strength with wondering fingers, drawn with him into ever-increasing circles of desire.

'Nick. . .' She moved her head restlessly, unable to articulate the depths of her need, but she felt him smile against the satiny skin of her stomach as he retraced his kisses with agonising slowness, lingering at the rosy swell of her breasts until she pleaded with him, her hands insistent against the hardness of him.

'*Please*, Nick. . .'

'Abby!' Nick's own breath was ragged. 'How could I ever have called you cold? You're all warmth. You're fire. . .sweet fire!'

Afterwards, he held her close while she drifted slowly down from sunbursts to the inexpressible comfort of his arms.

'I didn't know it could be like that,' she said quietly, when she could talk.

Nick turned his head, and for the first time she noticed the creases at the edges of his eyes. With one hand she touched them lightly, lovingly. His smile was alight with a warmth that set her heart pounding anew.

'I knew it would be with you,' he said, smoothing the hair from her forehead. 'I knew from the first moment I saw you standing by the side of the road. You had wild flowers all around you, and you stood there holding that beat-up old bike and looked down your nose at me. Nice nose, though!' He shifted slightly and searched her face with his eyes. '*Very* nice nose. Nice eyes, nice ears, nice mouth. . .' He dropped kisses as he went, light teasing kisses that moved lower and lower until Abby gasped in pleasure.

'You had the sun in your hair.' His lips drifted back to her throat. 'And you made me feel like a barbarian. Nobody had ever looked at me like that before. Your being Letty's neighbour was too good to be true. I was determined to get you to see me differently.'

'Are you sure you weren't just suffering from pique at finding someone who didn't fall at your feet?' Abby teased, rolling on top of him to begin her own delicious assault.

'A little, maybe. Not much. You were so patently unimpressed. The first time you smiled at me, really smiled at me, I felt as if I'd just won an Oscar!'

'Did you?' Abby's fingers were playing provocatively over the firm planes of his body, touching him, tasting him, as she kindled new fires. 'And what do you feel like now, Nicholas Carleton?'

Nick's smile as he swung her beneath him once more

set Abby's blood thudding in exquisite anticipation. 'Now? Now I feel like making love to you again. Do you have any objections, Miss Smith?'

'No,' Abby managed, between kisses. 'No objection at all.'

'How do you fancy a trip to London, honey?' Nick said to her as they lay in bed one afternoon. His fingers played idly with her hair.

'London?' Abby hesitated. 'What for?' She hated big cities and felt instinctively that things would be different there. The last few days had been blissful, just she and Nick alone with the rain beating against the windows, but now the sun was out once more, and the rest of the world threatened to intrude.

'*Tomorrow You Die* has been nominated for some awards at the new film festival. I promised I'd go to the ceremony.' He reached for her hand. 'I'd like you to be there, Abby.'

Abby didn't answer at once. She chewed her lip, grey eyes troubled.

'What's the problem?' Nick asked. 'Don't tell me you've got nothing to wear!'

'It's just. . .' She stared at him, hoping to make him understand. 'I'd be so out of place there,' she said eventually. 'It would be just like Washington. I've always hated parties. I never know what to say to people.'

'You've never had any trouble talking to me,' Nick pointed out.

'I know, but that's here. You're just. . .Nick. Will I have anything to say to Nicholas Carleton, superstar?'

'I'm the same man.' Nick swung himself off the bed impatiently and stepped into his trousers. 'I thought you of all people understood that.'

Abby drew the sheet round her as if she was cold. 'I just don't want to let you down,' she said in a low voice.

'How come you've got so little confidence in yourself?' he demanded. 'That guy Stephen really screwed you up, didn't he?' Nick stopped at the expression on her face. He sat down on the edge of the bed and pulled her close. 'Listen, haven't these last few days meant anything to you?'

'You know they have,' Abby whispered against his shoulder.

'Then trust me, Abby. Trust me to stay the same person wherever I am.'

Nick didn't refer to the awards ceremony again, but Abby sensed his disappointment and wished miserably that she had explained herself better. Stynch Magna was her whole life now, but for Nick it was just a summer holiday. He had never pretended that it was anything else, never mentioned what would happen when the holiday was over. He had an entire existence elsewhere that she knew nothing of, and where she probably had no place.

She thought about it now as she cycled along the main road to Turlbury. She had to deliver two long-overdue pictures to the dealer there, but then she would go back to Nick and talk to him properly. Perhaps she could prepare a nice meal, they could share a bottle of wine, and everything would be all right. He had told her to trust him, and she would.

Heartened at the prospect, Abby practised what she

would say all the way into town and could only offer preoccupied replies to the antiques dealer who wanted her opinion on another painting he had just acquired.

'What happened to that painting of Stynch Magna?' she asked him, suddenly struck by an idea. The house seemed to have associations with Nick now, and at the back of her mind was the thought that if she could keep the picture of it, she could keep part of Nick too.

'Sold.' The dealer beamed at her in satisfaction. 'Got a very good price for it too. You did a good job there, Abby.'

Her disappointment was silly, Abby reasoned to herself, as she hurried into the greengrocer's for some fresh vegetables. She wanted to get back to Nick as soon as possible, but once in the shop her mind went blank. What could she cook for him? She searched her memory feverishly for successful recipes as she peered over the display in the window. She made a distracted selection and was just trying to decide between strawberries and raspberries when a flash of familiar racing green in the road outside made her look up.

The Rolls was waiting at the red lights. With a sickening sense of unreality, Abby saw Nick turn to the woman beside him and put an arm round her shoulders while he waited for the lights to change. The woman rested her head against him, and then the light was green and the car was gone.

'Will there be anything else?' the shop assistant asked, puzzled by Abby's expression.

Numbly, Abby shook her head. She felt nothing, too shocked and hurt even for pain. As if in a dream, she paid and left the shop to stand staring after the car. It was long gone, of course, but the image of that blonde head leaning on Nick's shoulder was still vivid. There had been no mistaking the woman.

Charlotte Canning.

Nick had left a note on the kitchen table. It was very short. 'Have to go to London urgently. Back as soon as I can. Nick.' He had added as an afterthought, 'Trust me!'

Abby screwed up the piece of paper and dropped it in the bin. Trust him! Unwelcome feeling came flooding back with a savage rush, ripping and tearing the happiness of the last few days to bitter shreds. She had known how it would be. Why, why, why had she faced the truth about Nick and deliberately ignored it? Why had she turned aside from everything experience and Stephen had taught her to make a fool of herself again? She had no one to blame but herself. Her face burned with humiliation as she remembered how she had apologised to Nick after the fête. She had believed then that he was different from Stephen.

He *is* different, her heart whispered, but the memory of Charlotte Canning's blonde head on his shoulder told her differently. Well, what had she expected? Charlotte was part of his world in a way that Abby could never be—or would ever want to be, Abby added fiercely to herself. Nick had been amusing himself with her, no more. How could she have thought otherwise?

She refused to cry. She had cried enough over Stephen.

When Nick returned the next day, she was making pastry with ferocious concentration. She looked up briefly as he came into the kitchen, and tried to suppress the surge of emotion at the sight of him.

There were dark circles under his eyes, and he looked exhausted. Obviously Charlotte didn't allow him much sleep, thought Abby, hardening her heart.

'Hello, Abby,' Nick said quietly from the doorway.

'Hello.' Abby slapped the dough up and down on the board, refusing to meet his eyes, but Nick merely pulled out a chair on the other side of the table, and sat down where she couldn't avoid him.

'Take it easy on the dough, Abigail,' he said with a glimmering smile. 'What's it ever done to you?'

Abby's only reply was to pummel it even harder, so he went on, 'Aren't you going to ask where I've been?'

'You told me in the note. You've been to London. Bully for you.'

'All right, don't you want to know what I was doing?' Nick was being infuriatingly patient.

'I know what you were doing.' The dough was horribly over-worked by now, but Abby didn't care.

Nick lifted an eyebrow in surprise. 'You do?'

This time Abby looked him straight in the eye. 'I saw you driving off with Charlotte Canning, Nick.'

'That's not quite the same as knowing why I went, Abigail.'

'Let me guess. . .Charlotte crooked her little finger?' She turned away to scrabble through the kitchen drawers. 'Where *is* the bloody thing?' She slammed the drawers shut in frustration.

'What are you looking for?' Nick asked, diverted.

'The rolling-pin.' Abby felt tears perilously close.

'Is this it?' Nick picked up the rolling-pin from the table beside him, and Abby snatched it out of his hand, refusing to respond to his grin. She began to roll out the pastry with unnecessary force while the laughter faded from Nick's eyes.

'I'm sorry I couldn't ring you last night,' he tried again. 'I just didn't get a chance. I didn't get any sleep either.'

'I can imagine!'

Nick rubbed his eyes wearily. 'You think I went off with Charlotte, don't you?'

'You *did* go off with her. I saw her with my own eyes, if you remember!'

'Look, Abby, we've been through this before. Charlotte's a friend of mine. A good friend. She. . .needed me yesterday. I can't tell you why, because I promised that I wouldn't.'

The pastry had split irretrievably. Abby gathered it all up savagely and pounded it into a ball again. 'Really?'

'Really. Abby, I've been making love to you all week. Do you really think I'm likely to rush off and jump into bed with someone else?'

'I don't know.' Abby's hands stilled and she looked over the table at Nick. 'I really don't know. I don't know much about you, come to that. You come from a different world, Nick, and I don't belong there.'

'You could if you wanted to,' he said softly, but she just shook her head.

'Please believe me, Abby. I went to help Charlotte. I'm sorry I can't tell you why, but I shouldn't need to.' He paused. 'If you loved me, you wouldn't need to be told.'

Abby's lips trembled and she bent her head to the pastry again. 'I *don't* love you,' she lied.

'I think you do. You love me, but you don't trust

me.' Nick sighed. 'You can't have love without trust, Abby. I thought the problem was that I was American, but it's more than that, isn't it? You're right, I do come from a different world, but I'd like you to be part of it.' He leant over and clasped both her hands in his. 'I love you, Abby, but I can't give up the rest of my world for you. I wouldn't be me any more. Can you understand that?'

Abby nodded and he released her hands. They felt bereft without his touch.

'I guess you need to think.' Nick stood up. 'I'm going back to London, Abby. I'll leave you the name of my hotel but I won't try and persuade you to come with me. You need to work it out for yourself.'

Abby was struggling to keep back the tears. She felt miserably confused. Why couldn't he have been defensive, or even aggressive? She had wanted a furious argument, and instead he had sat there and *looked* like that, and she longed to throw herself into his arms and believe him. He had said he loved her, and her heart leapt at the thought. . .but Stephen had said he loved her too, hadn't he?

Nick came round the table and took her face gently between his hands, forcing her to look up into his eyes. They were warm and green and Abby could feel her resistance dissolve. 'You've got flour on your nose,' he murmured, and rubbed it off tenderly with his thumb. He bent his head to kiss her once, a brief, urgent kiss. 'Goodbye, Abigail Smith.' And then he had released her and was walking away. Abby wanted to call him back, but no words came.

He paused once, at the door. 'You do love me, you

know,' he said, his voice deep and rather uneven. The next moment he had gone.

Abby's knees trembled beneath her and she sat down abruptly on the nearest chair, her mind in a whirl of conflicting emotions. She did love him, Nick was right of course; she could run after him, but even as the thought beckoned, the images of Charlotte and Stephen circled mockingly.

'Oh, damn!' In a sudden burst of despair—with herself, with Nick, with Charlotte, with Stephen, with everything—Abby seized the beaten and battered lump of pastry and hurled it against the wall. It bounced off the paintwork and fell to the floor with a dull splat. Abby stared at it uncomprehendingly, and then buried her face into her hands and wept.

The cottage was achingly empty without Nick. Abby forced herself through the daily routine and suffered alone, with only her pride as a cold and cheerless comfort. She hadn't wanted to fall in love with Nick, all her instincts had been against it, but he had. . .he had *made* her! It was all his fault. He had set out to seduce her and she had fallen for all that charm and sincerity just like so many others before her. Hadn't she read all about that string of beautiful women he had been out with—or 'dated', as he would no doubt say? Was she really supposed to believe that, after all of them, Nick Carleton wanted plain Abigail Smith? Sometimes she stared at herself in the mirror, wondering what he had seen there. Her reflection looked pale and drawn and her grey eyes held a bruised look. He had wanted her for a few weeks, a few months perhaps, but how much longer? Film stars were not exactly noted for their fidelity. No, it was better this way. Abby gathered her remaining shreds of pride around her like a shield.

Liz was not fooled. 'You're letting stupid pride stand in the way of happiness. Don't try and tell me you don't love Nick—of course you do. And he loves you, Abby. He even told you so!' Liz was worried by the empty look in Abby's eyes, and worry made her cross. 'Though heaven knows why! You're so stiff-necked and stubborn, you don't deserve him.'

'If he loves me so much, why hasn't he come back?' Abby was provoked into replying. The question had nagged at her all week.

'Because until you decide to throw away all your prejudices against Americans and actors and all the other things that Nick happens to be, and just accept him for the man he is, there isn't any point in him coming back. You've got to trust him.' Liz unconsciously echoed Nick's words. 'You're being silly.' It was Liz's strongest criticism, but her face softened when she saw Abby's stricken expression.

'You can't shut yourself in here forever, Abby. There's a world out there, and you have to be part of it. Even Peter knows that much. He's accepted that he can't have you, so he's found someone else to bore. . .he now spends his whole time ogling Sarah over the counter in the shop, and getting every encouragement! Poor old Geoff's taking it badly.' Liz paused and said gently. 'You see, you're not the only one, Abby. If you won't go to Nick, you've got to start making your own life again. You can start by coming round to supper. You don't look as if you're eating enough.'

Abby didn't want to eat, but she went round to Liz

anyway that evening. The cottage echoed with memories of Nick, and her friend's vehemence had thrown her into confusion once more. Liz cooked a delicious supper and Abby made a tremendous effort to be good company, unaware that her smile was over-bright and her chatter too forced. Liz and Mike pretended not to notice, but no one objected when Mike suggested that they watch the evening news with their coffee.

Abby stared at the television, watching the newsreaders' mouths open and close and hearing nothing. Was Liz right about Nick? She ached to have him beside her, to be able to turn to him and touch him and see the smile lurking in his eyes. She pressed the back of her hand to her mouth so that Liz would not see her lips trembling, and as she did so Nick's face appeared on the screen so unexpectedly that she jerked back as if she had been burnt.

'—las Carleton. Stars of stage and screen are gathering in London for the international awards ceremony which takes place tomorrow night. Also tipped for an award is Carleton's co-star, Charlotte Canning, who today announced her engagement to Senator Dale Gray.' A picture flashed up of Charlotte walking into a famous hotel with a distinguished-looking man of about forty-five. They both smiled for the cameras, but hurried past the crowd of reporters without speaking, and the voice-over continued, 'Miss Canning refused to comment on the news that her brother is being held for questioning following the seizure of drugs at Heathrow last week. Major British hopes for an award centre on. . .' The voice droned on, but Abby was no longer listening.

Charlotte Canning—engaged?

Nick's voice rang clearly in her memory. 'Charlotte's a friend of mine. A good friend.' He would have gone to help her if her brother was in trouble. Why hadn't she believed him? She was still as blind and prejudiced as Liz said she was.

Liz was watching her with concern. 'You see, he wasn't lying,' she said gently.

'No.' Abby swallowed. 'You were right, Liz, I've been so stupid. But it's too late now.'

'What do you mean?'

'He wouldn't want to see me now, not after I've been so pig-headed. . .would he?' She looked appealingly at Liz.

'There's only one way to find out.'

Abby's fingers fumbled with the change as the taxi drew up outside the hotel. 'Here you are, love.' The taxi-driver turned round and grinned at her, and Abby smiled back weakly, grateful for his cheerful friendliness. London was overwhelmingly noisy and busy after Stynch Magna and she was reluctant to leave the security of the taxi.

Was she making a terrible mistake, thinking that she could become part of Nick's life in a place like this? If London was bad, how would she cope with Los Angeles or New York? Her nerve almost failed her, but the taxi-driver was looking at her expectantly, so she paid him and stepped out on to the pavement. The hotel loomed intimidatingly in front of her, and it took all Abby's courage to walk up to the reception desk and ask for Nick.

The supercilious young man behind the desk gave her a suspicious look, and for the first time Abby realised that all sorts of people must try and wangle their way in to see him. The young man opened his mouth to deny her, but she interrupted him, suddenly terrified that she would be turned away after having got so far.

'Oh, please, I'm not. . .it's just that it's terribly important that I see him. I know he's here.' She fished desperately in her bag for the scrap of paper Nick had left with the name of the hotel on it, but could find nothing except old shopping-lists and receipts. She raised despairing eyes to the receptionist. '*Please*, if you could just say that Abigail Smith is here?'

Perhaps there was something in her face, but the young man unbent sufficiently to offer her a chilly smile. 'I'll see if Mr Carleton is available.' He turned away to murmur into a telephone, and when he turned back his look was speculative.

'Mr Carleton has asked me to tell you not to move!'

'Thank you,' Abby whispered, her heart pounding so loudly that she was sure everyone in the hotel must hear it. She turned to face the crowded foyer apprehensively, her handbag clutched in front of her as if her life depended upon it.

Expensively dressed women drifted past her and Abby's heart sank. She was wearing the simple blue and green dress she had worn to the fête, and her hair was loose about her shoulders. She had thought she looked all right in Stynch Magna, but here in this elegant hotel she felt woefully inadequate. Nick would take one look at her and turn away in disgust!

She had been mad to think he might want anything to do with her, Abby realised desperately. She was so dowdy. She was narrow-minded and pig-headed and awkward. She could never fit into his sophisticated life, never! In a sudden panic, she glanced over at the lifts. There was no sign of Nick. She could slip away. . .but she had sidled no more than ten steps towards the doors when a voice yelled across the foyer.

'Abigail Smith! You stay right there!'

Everyone, including Abby, turned to stare. Nick was running down the stairs, pausing for breath at the last turn, careless of all the faces upturned below him.

'I can see you,' he panted furiously. 'Don't you dare run away!'

He began to leap down the final flight of steps three at a time, but his momentum carried him straight into a matronly woman laden with carrier-bags who was just about to start up the stairs. The resultant collision left shopping strewn around them, although miraculously the woman managed to keep on her feet.

'I'm so sorry, ma'am!' Apologising profusely, one eye on Abby, Nick bent to pick up the bags.

Abby did not wait to see any more. Nerve broken, she turned and hurried for the door.

CHAPTER TEN

'ABBY!' Nick thrust the shopping back at the unfortunate woman and came after her, ignoring his interested audience.

Once outside, Abby looked wildly about her before plunging into the crowds. Half walking, half running, she glanced back over her shoulder to see the doorman pointing her out to Nick.

Traitor, she thought bitterly, as her eyes met Nick's over the heads of the passers-by. His look told her that there was no escape. Abby hesitated, took a few steps backwards, then stopped, her shoulders slumping in defeat. This was stupid!

'Come back here right now!' Nick was shouting. He began to push his way towards her, but less frantically now that he could see that she was not going anywhere.

Abby still held her bag defensively against her chest and she swallowed nervously as Nick seized her and pulled her to one side of the pavement. He looked blazingly angry.

'What do you think you're doing?' He was still trying to catch his breath. 'I just ran down twelve storeys of that damn hotel, and you ran away! I ought to beat you!' He glared down at her before jerking her into his arms and kissing her hard. '*Now* I'm going to beat you!' he threatened somewhat shakily when he released her. Both of them were breathless, and Abby stared indignantly back up at him, thoroughly ruffled.

She had expected coolness, resentment, even hostility, not this bright-eyed, jubilant anger. She had imagined talking things through in a mature adult way, not being chased along the street or manhandled in full view of London!

Nick looked down at Abby's bag still jammed uncomfortably between them and grabbed it out of her hands. 'What have you got in here?'

'It's just my bag.' Abby tried to take it back but he held it out of her reach.

'Uh-uh. You won't be able to go anywhere without your handbag. I know women. I'll take it. You come along with me.'

With her bag held ridiculously in one hand, Nick dragged Abby back to the hotel so that she had to run to keep up with him. Indifferent to the curious looks they were receiving, he pulled her over to the lifts and jabbed the call button. 'I'm not going up those stairs again!' He was still breathing heavily.

Horribly conscious of numerous interested and amused eyes upon her, Abby stared desperately at the lift doors, praying that it would come quickly.

Nick still held her hand tightly. 'I don't understand you, Abigail. You come up to London, you ask to see me, and then when I appear, you run away. What did you do that for?' he demanded in a loud voice, and Abby cast him a glance of agonised embarrassment.

'Ssh! Everybody's looking at us!' she muttered out of the side of her mouth.

'Sure they're looking at us! And why are they doing that, Abigail? Because *you* ran off! So don't tell me to "ssh"!' Nick jabbed at the button again. 'Where's the damn lift?'

To Abby's unutterable relief the doors slid open at that moment and he pulled her inside. There were several people in the lift, but Nick took not the slightest bit of notice, continuing to harangue her until Abby's own anger began to get the better of her embarrassment.

'Let me go!' she spat. 'I certainly didn't come to London to be embarrassed and humiliated like this!'

'What did you come for, then? I've been sitting by the phone waiting for you to call all week, and then when you finally turn up you disappear as soon as I get there. Was a glimpse of you across the lobby supposed to be all I was going to get?' he asked sarcastically. 'Big of you, Abigail!'

The other passengers were studiously watching the illuminated lights above the doors as the lift slid upwards with hideous slowness.

'There was no need for you to yell and carry on like that,' she whispered furiously. 'It was so embarrassing! Anyone would think you were in that ghastly television show of yours that everyone goes on about. What's it called? *Carter*?'

'*Carver*! For someone who's never watched it, you seem to know a lot about it,' Nick flashed back, 'and it is not *ghastly*!'

'It's excellent,' an anonymous voice proffered from the back of the lift, and Nick shot her a triumphant look.

'Hear that? Funny how only Abigail thinks it's *ghastly*! Abigail, who has never watched one of my shows!'

'If I'd known it was so important to you that I waste

my time watching a lot of rubbish on television, then I *would* have watched one!' Abby snapped.

'Oh, we couldn't have that. You might have been forced to voice an opinion on something you actually knew about!'

'Oh, shut up!' Abby glared at the sarcasm in his voice. 'And give me back my bag!'

'No way. I haven't finished with you yet.'

'Well, I've finished with *you*!'

'Is that what you came up to London to say?'

Green eyes stared angrily into grey in the suddenly taut silence. The other passengers had given up the pretence of not listening and were looking on with interest, but Abby was no longer aware of them. She opened her mouth to say yes, but no words would come, and she could only stare helplessly back at Nick as the anger faded from his face and a different light began to glow in his eyes.

The lift doors opened noiselessly on to a long, empty corridor. 'This is us,' Nick said and pulled Abby unprotesting out of the lift. He looked back as the doors were closing. 'Sorry, folks, that's the end of this week's episode.'

They were left alone in the muffled silence of thick carpets and subdued lighting, and now Abby couldn't meet his eyes. Her fury had dissolved as quickly as it had flared, and she was conscious only of a terrible longing and the sinking realisation that she had ruined everything.

'Come on,' Nick said quietly and without speaking they walked down the long corridor to his room. Abby found herself in a vast, luxurious suite while Nick closed the door firmly behind him and tossed her bag on to a table. Nervously, she walked over to the window and stood fiddling with her watch strap and looking out over the park. It was packed with office workers enjoying their sandwiches in the late summer sunshine.

'Abby?' She could feel Nick's eyes upon her, could hear him crossing the room to stand next to her.

'Yes?' It was hardly more than a whisper.

'Did you really come to tell me we were finished?'

'No.' Abby drew a deep breath and turned to him. 'No. I came to tell you that I'd been wrong about everything and. . .and to tell you that I was sorry. Again. I know I've said I was sorry before, but it wasn't until I saw the news about Charlotte and her brother that I realised quite how stupid I'd been. That was the reason you went to London with Charlotte that time?'

He nodded. 'Charlotte was in a pretty bad way. She was worried sick about Kevin—that's her brother—and I was the only real friend she had to turn to over here. She just turned up on the doorstep that day, and she was in such a state, I took her straight back to London. What a mess! Kev's always been wild, but he's gone too far this time. We had to go and see him at the police station, then talk to the US Consul and fix up an attorney. It wasn't too much fun. I guess Charlotte hoped it would all turn out to be a mistake and that the matter would be dropped quietly. That's why she begged me not to tell anyone—even you.'

'I see.'

'You know what?' he went on. 'Charlotte was worried about her brother, but she was even more worried about telling Dale. He wanted to marry her, and she thought if the news got out, it would be bad for his political career.' He shook his head. 'How can you be so dumb? As if a man like Dale would put his career before Charlotte! I made her ring him, and of course he flew right over.'

'She didn't trust him,' Abby whispered.

'That's right. But she does now. They got to have a happy ending.'

Abby could feel the tears standing on the ends of her lashes and tried to blink them back. He had sorted out Charlotte's happy ending only to go back to another stupidly distrustful woman. Instead of the warm welcome he'd deserved, he'd had all her prejudices thrown in his face—again.

'And what about us, Abby? Are we going to have a happy ending?'

She was fighting a losing battle against the tears. 'Oh, Nick, I've been so awful to you!' A large drop trickled down her face and she wiped it away hastily. 'I spent all those weeks telling myself you were just like Stephen, and pretending that I hated you because you were American, but it was just a defence. It took me so long to get over Stephen and losing the baby and everything. I'd just built myself a cosy little life in Stynch Magna and I thought it was all I wanted, and then you came along and confused me.' She was weeping openly now. 'I did everything not to fall in love with you, Nick. I didn't want to give up my security and to have to take chances on people again. When I saw you with Charlotte, I suppose I thought I'd been justified in resisting you all along, but of course it was too late by then.'

'Too late?'

'Of course, I'd fallen in love with you!' she said almost angrily. 'And I didn't want my cosy little life any more. It wasn't really you I didn't trust, Nick. I didn't trust myself to know what I really wanted.'

'Do you know what you want now, Abby?' Nick's voice was oddly husky and at last she looked straight at him.

'I want you. I want you and your awful shirts and your whistling and your irritating habit of always jumping over things.' She sniffed back the tears unromantically and tried to smile. 'I even want your American accent and the way you say "Monday thru Friday" and "I guess" the whole time. I want to be part of your life wherever you are.'

'Hey!' Nick couldn't prevent the grin spreading across his face. 'You really do love me!' Abby nodded against his chest as his arms closed around her. 'Go on, Abby, say it.'

'I love you, Nick.'

He tangled his fingers in her silky hair and turned her face up to his. Abby felt a dawning sense of incredulous happiness at the warm light in his green eyes. 'I love you too, Abby,' he said softly.

'But Nick, I've been so rude and hurtful and distrustful. You need someone sweet and kind who'll watch all your shows and never criticise you for mispronouncing aluminium.'

'No, I don't. I need you, Abby.' He bent his head until their lips were just touching. 'And *you're* the one who can't say aluminum properly!'

Abby's only reply was to slip her hands round his neck and pull him closer. Their kiss was deep and warm as she melted into the lean strength of his body and his hands slid over her back, pressing her nearer still.

'Oh, Abby,' Nick almost groaned, burying his face against her hair at last. 'I missed you so much, honey.' He swung her up and carried her over to the sofa to settle her comfortably on his lap. 'You don't know how much I missed you. I kept thinking about you and wishing you were here. It's no fun being an American without you to irritate!'

'I always did think you just did it all to annoy,' Abby said, kissing his neck where the pulse beat steadily beneath his ear, and then teasing a trail with her lips and tongue to his throat. She felt an almost delirious happiness bubbling within her.

'At least you won't be able to complain about my clothes any more. Who'd have thought that you'd come to love my shirts as well as me? And don't try to deny it, Abigail—you said you wanted me *and* my shirts!'

'I can't have been thinking straight,' she explained and kissed his ear. 'Can't I take it back?'

'Nope. Love me, love my wardrobe.' His arms tightened around her. 'You gave me a bad moment that day when you told me you didn't love me.'

Abby pulled away slightly to look at him. 'I was lying. You knew that.'

'I thought I did. But then you didn't come and you didn't come, and I got to thinking, why should a girl like that love me? You were so cool and stylish. No wonder you hated my clothes.'

'Stylish!' Abby gave a peal of laughter. 'Everyone's always telling me how frumpish and old-fashioned I am!'

'Old-fashioned, perhaps, but never frumpish, Abby! You've got your own style. Remember that first time we met and I called you duchess? That's how I think of you. When I'm with you, I feel like a king. I know that everyone else is thinking, "What's that beautiful girl doing with a jerk like that?" but I think I'm the only one who knows how warm and vulnerable you are underneath. That's why I couldn't take you seriously when you said that you'd never be able to fit into my world. I'd be so proud to be seen with you.'

'Oh, Nick.' Abby leant her cheek against his. 'I couldn't believe you'd be interested in me when you know so many beautiful, glamorous women. I'm so ordinary.'

'No one who can stand up for rabbits' rights is that ordinary. You're the squarest girl I ever met, and the best.'

She kissed him again then. Their kiss deepened and became more exciting until they slid together to lie on the sofa. Nick's fingers were at the buttons at the front of her dress, slipping it off her shoulders and brushing aside her flimsy bra.

His mouth followed his hands in a devastating exploration, teasing and sucking until Abby sobbed with pleasure and moved restlessly beneath him. When he stripped off his own clothes, she welcomed him back into her arms, revelling in the feel and the taste of him.

Whispering soft words of love, they kissed and touched with increasing urgency until Abby thought that she would dissolve with wanting him. She gasped his name, breathless with desire, needing him closer, closer, and, together at last, they soared to unimagined heights that left them trembling with ecstasy in each other's arms.

Later, much later, when Nick was running his hands possessively over the warm curves of her body, and telling her exactly which he loved most, and why, the phone rang. With a sigh, he rolled over, taking Abby with him, and picked up the receiver.

'Yes? Oh, Charlotte.' His hold on Abby tightened as her own hands drifted over his hard stomach. 'Oh, you heard about the scene in the lobby, did you? Yes, she is here, and, no, this isn't a good time to call!. . .It's *what* time?' He sat up suddenly. 'I'd forgotten all about it!' He put his hand over the receiver and rolled his eyes at Abby. 'We're supposed to be leaving for the awards ceremony in an hour! Have you got anything to wear?'

'Only what I came in.' Abby glanced over to where her dress lay in a discarded heap by the sofa. 'I can't go in that!'

'Well, I'm sure as hell not going without you.' Nick took his hand away and explained the situation rapidly to Charlotte. There was a pause while he listened and then he said, 'Great. See you then,' and put down the phone.

'Charlotte's going to lend you a dress,' he explained. 'She's going to come round when she's finished getting ready.' He swung Abby beneath him once more. 'But, knowing Charlotte, that may be some time. We'll just have to think of some way to occupy ourselves until she turns up.'

'Shouldn't we have a shower or something?' Abby suggested, without much conviction, already quivering at his touch.

Nick pretended to consider but his hands were destroying any last thoughts of resistance or common sense. 'Let's start with "something", shall we?'

When Charlotte swept into the suite some forty minutes later, Abby was contemplating her reflection rather dubiously. With a large towel wrapped round her and her hair hanging damply to her shoulders, it seemed impossible that she would ever be ready. But Charlotte was undeterred.

'You're going to look stunning! I've got just the right dress for you, Abigail. Isn't it lucky we're about the same size?'

Abby remembered Charlotte's eclipsing beauty, but she was unprepared for her warmth and friendliness.

'It's very kind of you,' she said shyly, as Charlotte waved Nick out of the room and directed a porter to deposit what seemed an enormous pile of dresses on the sofa.

'Don't be silly, darling. This is fun!'

She inspected Abby critically before sitting her down in front of the mirror and drying her hair with deft professionalism. 'I used to be a hairdresser before I got my break into movies,' she confessed. 'You can tell a lot about a woman from her hair.' She laughed at Abby's surprise. 'People always think movie stars live in a sort of fantasy world, but we're all very ordinary underneath.'

She left Abby's hair loose, tumbling in a shining mass to her shoulders, and then made her sit perfectly still while she made up her face. Abby hardly recognised herself when she had finished. Her eyes looked huge and brilliant, the fine bones cleverly emphasised with the subtle use of blusher, the generous mouth dramatically coloured.

'Oh!' was all she could say.

Charlotte stood back to admire her handiwork. 'I'd like to say it was all my own work, but I didn't do much. You've just got such a glow about you. . .and I guess that owes more to Nick than to make-up!'

The two women's eyes met in the mirror and they exchanged a smile of understanding.

'I'm so sorry about your brother,' Abby said impulsively. 'Nick told me what happened.'

Charlotte began putting the make-up away in a huge box. 'Kev's not really bad. He's just a bit wild. I think maybe he's learnt his lesson—he didn't feel quite so clever when he was sitting in a police cell. Now we just have to wait and see what kind of sentence he gets.' She shrugged. 'It was just lucky I happened to be in England at the same time, but I had no idea what to do. I don't know what I'd have done without Nick. He dealt with everything. And if it hadn't been for him, I'd never have called Dale. I owe him a lot.' She looked back at Abby as she closed the lid of the box. 'Nick's a good man, Abby.'

'I know.' Abby flushed slightly. 'Did he tell you how jealous I was of you?'

'No, really?' Charlotte gave a peal of laughter. 'If only you know how much I've had to hear about *you*! I've never known Nick to be boring before.' She paused. 'I'm real glad you came, Abby. He's been pretty unhappy this last week and tonight especially it'll mean so much to have you with him. You know he's up for an award?'

'Will he win?'

'He sure deserves to, but he probably won't care now you're here.' Charlotte leant forward and put her hand over Abby's. 'Seriously, Abby, you don't ever need to be jealous of me, or of anyone else. Nick has this playboy image, but he's square as a box really. . .strictly a one-woman man!'

Abby gave a tremulous smile. 'Thank you, Charlotte—for everything.'

Charlotte waved her hand in a dismissive gesture. 'What are friends for? Hey, we haven't time to sit here talking!' She jumped up gaily. 'We've got to get you dressed!'

She held up a shimmering creation in midnight-blue. 'Perfect!' It slithered over Abby's head with a seductive whisper of silk and she turned slowly in front of the mirror, watching the way the skirt billowed and floated around her legs. It fell in a swirl of blue from a tight bodice which left her shoulders bare.

'I feel naked,' she said with a little laugh.

'That's how you're supposed to feel,' Charlotte said with a knowing grin. 'You're going to slay them all tonight.'

'Are you girls ready yet?' Nick demanded, appearing in the bedroom doorway. He was shrugging himself into his dinner-jacket but stopped dead when he saw Abby standing almost shyly by the mirror.

At the sight of him, Abby felt her heart turn over. He looked devastatingly attractive in the formal black and white, but it was the smile that began in his eyes that melted her bones and set her tingling with desire.

'You look. . .beautiful!' he breathed, starting towards her.

'Don't mess her hair!' They had both forgotten

Charlotte, who put her hands on her hips in a mock threatening pose. 'I know what you guys want to do, but we've got a party to go to. I'm not collecting that award for you, Nick, and I'm not leaving you alone either, so you can take that look out of your eyes!'

Nick grinned reluctantly as he walked over to Abby and took both her hands. 'I suppose I can't mess your lipstick either?'

Abby's eyes said that she wouldn't mind, but Charlotte said sharply, 'Absolutely not!' so he pressed a warm kiss on each palm instead.

'You're very lovely, duchess. Do you really love me?'

Abby nodded with shining eyes, before Charlotte interrupted again. 'OK, that's enough. Come on, you guys, we're going to be late as it is!'

Nick gave up with a laugh. 'We'd better go, or she'll never leave us alone. But I warn you, we're coming home early!'

For Abby the evening passed in a blur of popping lights and champagne corks. Around her the tables glittered with silver, crystal and expensive jewellery, but she was conscious only of Nick sitting close beside her, his hand warm on her thigh through the silk. They talked and laughed with the other guests, but both thought only of the time they would be alone together again.

'I worked it out,' Nick whispered in her ear. 'At the earliest we can leave in one hour forty-three and a half minutes.'

An expectant hush fell over the gathering as the presentation began. Abby found herself watching Nick's face magnified on the special screen as they played clips from the nominated films. She studied it as if he were a stranger, realising for the first time that, although the features were the same, the man on the screen was not the man she loved. The celluloid smile was attractive, but it was not the warm, crooked smile he kept for her. On screen, he was the character he played, off screen he was Nick, sitting beside her now and whispering again, 'Only one hour twenty-seven minutes to go.'

She held his hand tightly as the envelope was opened with agonising deliberation and then a great cheer went up. 'The Award for Best Actor goes to. . .Nick Carleton!'

'It's you!' Abby clapped her hands with delight and he kissed her in front of everybody before standing up. She watched him weave his way through the tables, acknowledging the applause and shaking hands as he went, and felt as if she would burst with pride.

Charlotte leant across the table. 'Are you still sorry I dragged you away from the hotel?'

'No, I'm so happy for him. And you were right, he had to collect the award himself.'

They both looked over to where Nick was finishing his speech of thanks. 'But now that he's done it,' said Charlotte, 'I don't suppose anyone will mind if you leave early!'

Nick's first words as he slid back into his seat were in an undertone to Abby—'One hour sixteen minutes!'—but in fact it was something less than that when he took her hand and they slipped away through the crowds, avoiding the press of photographers, and back to the hotel. The foyer was mercifully quiet and the receptionist poker-faced as he handed Nick the key.

They had the lift to themselves this time. As soon as the doors closed, Nick took her in his arms and they kissed hungrily as if they had been apart for days.

'Come on.' Nick's voice was husky as the doors slid open. 'Let's get to the room and hang out the "Do Not Disturb" sign!'

But when they stepped out they found themselves face to face with the receptionist once more. 'What are we doing here?' Nick demanded, puzzled. 'I thought we were on the twelfth floor.'

The receptionist looked them up and down, taking in Abby's dishevelled hair and Nick with his bow-tie askew and lipstick on his collar. 'You need to push the button for the floor you require, sir,' he pointed out with an air of patient long-suffering. 'Otherwise the lift will remain where it is.'

'Sure, thanks.' It was the first time Abby had seen Nick embarrassed, and she began to giggle as they got back into the lift. Nick pushed the button marked 'twelve' with great deliberation with a last wave at the receptionist, and then he too began to laugh. They were still laughing as they fell into the suite, and Nick locked the door firmly behind them.

'At last,' he said, advancing towards her with determination. 'I've been thinking about this moment all evening. I thought it was never going to end.'

'I know,' said Abby when she could. 'But I'm glad we went. I'm so proud of you, Nick.'

He took the statue from his pocket and put it on the mantelpiece. 'It's just something extra to dust,' he joked, but she could tell he was pleased. 'And, talking of dusting, I have something for you.'

He drew a flat package from a drawer and handed it

to her. 'For me?' Abby weighed it in her hands. 'It feels like a picture.'

'Open it.'

It was the painting of Stynch Manor she had cleaned so lovingly. 'Oh, Nick!' She looked at him, her eyes starry with delight, and then back to the painting. 'I was so disappointed when I heard it had been sold. I never dreamt you had bought it!'

'That's not the only thing you'll have to dust,' Nick went on, obviously pleased at her reaction. He turned the picture over in her hands and showed her the envelope taped to the back.

'What's this?' Carefully Abby put the painting down and opened the envelope, pulling out a stiff legal document. Her eyes began to scan the close type until she came across something that made her stop and stare at Nick. 'These are the deeds to Stynch Manor!'

He took the paper out of her suddenly nerveless fingers. 'I bought it for you, Abby.'

'F-for me?'

'Well, for us.' Nick's arms closed round her and he held her tightly against him so that she could hear his heart beating through his shirt. 'I always used to accuse you of being an old-fashioned girl, but I guess I'm old-fashioned too. I never wanted to get married until I found the right girl, and now I have.' He held her a little way from him so that he could look down into her face. '*Will* you marry me, Abby?'

For a moment Abby was too happy to speak, and then she smiled, her warmest and truest smile. 'Of course I will.'

The astonishingly anxious expression on Nick's face dissolved with an answering smile of relief. 'You will?'

He pulled her close once more. 'I was always going to come back for you, you see. I hoped against hope you'd trust me enough to come, but if you hadn't I'd have been back to get you anyway.' He laid his cheek against her hair. 'I know how hard it will be for you to give up your village life for mine. But, wherever we go, I want us to have Stynch Manor to come home to. Much as I like your cottage, it's not really big enough for a family, is it?'

He cupped her face in his strong hands. 'Hey, you're not crying, are you? Is it the thought of all that dusting?'

Abby laughed through tears of happiness. 'I'll love the dusting,' she promised as Nick wiped her cheeks with his thumbs.

'I'll remind you of that in ten years' time!' he said. 'I couldn't forget your face as you walked round that house. It was as if it was built for you. I decided to buy it there and then, in spite of everything your friend Peter said to dissuade me.'

'But you were so cold to me that day!'

'*You* were cold,' Nick corrected. 'I knew I'd found the girl I'd been looking for for so long, but every time I thought I was getting close to you you'd slap me down. I thought you'd never have anything to do with an American, but I bought the house anyway—just in case! If the worst came to the worst, I'd still have an excuse to come back and see you.'

Abby spread her fingers against the solid warmth of his chest and looked into his eyes, suddenly serious. 'I don't deserve all this, Nick.'

'I know you don't,' he said, deliberately misunderstanding. 'You don't deserve to end up in a tumbledown house with a—what was it you called me once?—oh, yes, a loud, brash American for a husband. . .but do you think you could learn to put up with him, Abigail Smith?'

'On two conditions.'

'What are they?' He was dropping kisses along the pure line of her shoulder, and she shivered with desire as she began to unbutton his shirt.

'One, that you stop calling me Abigail Smith, and two, that you take me to bed now and make love to me all night!'

Nick's grin was jubilant as he swung her into his arms, kissed her and headed for the bedroom. 'You got it—Abigail Carleton!'

HARLEQUIN

Romance

A Christmas tradition...

Imagine spending Christmas in New
Orleans with a blind stranger and his aged
guide dog—when you're supposed to be
there on your honeymoon!
#3163 Every Kind of Heaven
by Bethany Campbell

Imagine spending Christmas with a man
you once "married"—in a mock ceremony
at the age of eight!
#3166 The Forgetful Bride
by Debbie Macomber

*Available in December 1991, wherever
Harlequin books are sold.*

RXM

HISTORICAL

CHRISTMAS

STORIES · 1991

Bring back heartwarming memories of Christmas past,
with Historical Christmas Stories 1991, a collection of
romantic stories by three popular authors:

Christmas Yet To Come
by Lynda Trent
A Season of Joy
by Caryn Cameron
Fortune's Gift
by DeLoras Scott
A perfect Christmas gift!

H A R L E Q U I N

Romance

This December, travel to
Northport, Massachusetts,
with Harlequin Romance
FIRST CLASS title #3164,
A TOUCH OF FORGIVENESS
by Emma Goldrick

Folks in Northport called Kitty the meanest woman in town,
but she couldn't forget how they had duped her brother and
exploited her family's land. It was hard to be mean, though,
when Joel Carmody was around—his calm, good humor
made Kitty feel like a new woman. Nevertheless, a Carmody
was a Carmody, and the name meant money and power to
the townspeople.... Could Kitty really trust Joel, or was he
like all the rest?

HARLEQUIN
PROUDLY PRESENTS
A DAZZLING NEW CONCEPT IN ROMANCE FICTION

One small town—twelve terrific love stories

Welcome to Tyler, Wisconsin—a town full of people
you'll enjoy getting to know, memorable friends and
unforgettable lovers, and a long-buried secret that
lurks beneath its serene surface....

JOIN US FOR A YEAR IN THE LIFE OF
TYLER

Each book set in Tyler is a self-contained love story;
together, the twelve novels stitch the fabric of a
community.

LOSE YOUR HEART TO TYLER!

The excitement begins in March 1992, with
WHIRLWIND, by Nancy Martin. When lively, brash
Liza Baron arrives home unexpectedly, she moves
into the old family lodge, where the silent and
mysterious Cliff Forrester has been living in seclusion
for years....

WATCH FOR ALL TWELVE BOOKS
OF THE TYLER SERIES
Available wherever Harlequin books are sold

TYLER-G

"INDULGE A LITTLE" SWEEPSTAKES

HERE'S HOW THE SWEEPSTAKES WORKS

NO PURCHASE NECESSARY

To enter each drawing, complete the appropriate Official Entry Form or a 3" by 5" index card by hand-printing your name, address and phone number and the trip destination that the entry is being submitted for (i.e., Walt Disney World Vacation Drawing, etc.) and mailing it to: Indulge '91 Subscribers-Only Sweepstakes, P.O. Box 1397, Buffalo, New York 14269-1397.

No responsibility is assumed for lost, late or misdirected mail. Entries must be sent separately with first class postage affixed, and be received by: 9/30/91 for the Walt Disney World Vacation Drawing, 10/31/91 for the Alaskan Cruise Drawing and 11/30/91 for the Hawaiian Vacation Drawing. Sweepstakes is open to residents of the U.S. and Canada, 21 years of age or older as of 11/7/91.

For complete rules, send a self-addressed, stamped (WA residents need not affix return postage) envelope to: Indulge '91 Subscribers-Only Sweepstakes Rules, P.O. Box 4005, Blair, NE 68009.

© 1991 HARLEQUIN ENTERPRISES LTD.

DIR-RL

"INDULGE A LITTLE" SWEEPSTAKES

HERE'S HOW THE SWEEPSTAKES WORKS

NO PURCHASE NECESSARY

To enter each drawing, complete the appropriate Official Entry Form or a 3" by 5" index card by hand-printing your name, address and phone number and the trip destination that the entry is being submitted for (i.e., Walt Disney World Vacation Drawing, etc.) and mailing it to: Indulge '91 Subscribers-Only Sweepstakes, P.O. Box 1397, Buffalo, New York 14269-1397.

No responsibility is assumed for lost, late or misdirected mail. Entries must be sent separately with first class postage affixed, and be received by: 9/30/91 for the Walt Disney World Vacation Drawing, 10/31/91 for the Alaskan Cruise Drawing and 11/30/91 for the Hawaiian Vacation Drawing. Sweepstakes is open to residents of the U.S. and Canada, 21 years of age or older as of 11/7/91.

For complete rules, send a self-addressed, stamped (WA residents need not affix return postage) envelope to: Indulge '91 Subscribers-Only Sweepstakes Rules, P.O. Box 4005, Blair, NE 68009.

© 1991 HARLEQUIN ENTERPRISES LTD.

DIR-RL

INDULGE A LITTLE—WIN A LOT!

Summer of '91 Subscribers-Only Sweepstakes

OFFICIAL ENTRY FORM

This entry must be received by: Nov. 30, 1991
This month's winner will be notified by: Dec. 7, 1991
Trip must be taken between: Jan. 7, 1992—Jan. 7, 1993

YES, I want to win the 3-Island Hawaiian vacation for two. I understand the prize includes round-trip airfare, first-class hotels and pocket money as revealed on the "wallet" scratch-off card.

Name _____

Address_____ Apt. _____

City _____

State/Prov. _____ Zip/Postal Code _____

Daytime phone number _____
(Area Code)

Return entries with invoice in envelope provided. Each book in this shipment has two entry coupons—and the more coupons you enter, the better your chances of winning!

© 1991 HARLEQUIN ENTERPRISES LTD.   3R-CPS

INDULGE A LITTLE—WIN A LOT!

Summer of '91 Subscribers-Only Sweepstakes

OFFICIAL ENTRY FORM

This entry must be received by: Nov. 30, 1991
This month's winner will be notified by: Dec. 7, 1991
Trip must be taken between: Jan. 7, 1992—Jan. 7, 1993

YES, I want to win the 3-Island Hawaiian vacation for two. I understand the prize includes round-trip airfare, first-class hotels and pocket money as revealed on the "wallet" scratch-off card.

Name _____

Address_____ Apt. _____

City _____

State/Prov. _____ Zip/Postal Code _____

Daytime phone number _____
(Area Code)

Return entries with invoice in envelope provided. Each book in this shipment has two entry coupons—and the more coupons you enter, the better your chances of winning!

© 1991 HARLEQUIN ENTERPRISES LTD.   3R-CPS